A SECOND SPARK

THE WAITE BROTHERS BOOK TWO

ANGEL DEVLIN

Cover by Shower of Schmidt designs

SUMMARY

When the light of your life flickers out, can a compassionate electrician reignite the spark?

One tragic day brings Becca Staveley to her knees, her beloved husband gone. But her nightmare is just beginning as secrets from his past threaten everything she's ever known.

Callum Waite has secrets of his own. Closed off from love, he feels more comfortable rewiring houses than fixing hearts. But he can't forget the girl he met years ago, and as Becca slowly begins to heal, the ice around Callum's heart begins to thaw.

He's exactly what Becca needs, and she's everything Callum didn't know he wanted; but can they survive what life has thrown at them and get another chance at love?

CHAPTER ONE

Becca

"Too late, you have my ring on your finger now, Princess." I heard Milo Waite bellow, his voice carrying through my open kitchen window. I couldn't see anything for the privet hedge that ran between our properties, but I knew Milo had moved in next door today. My neighbour and newest friend, Violet, had got engaged yesterday after a whirlwind romance with the man who lived in the house across the garden from her.

It's funny how you don't really know the community around you. I'd recently found out about the Waite family. Five brothers and one sister and a whole load of skeletons in the closet.

They lived on the next street. Juliet Waite, the lone female of the family, had spent last night—after celebrating with one too many glasses of wine—telling me all about their newly discovered half-sibling.

"Oh for a boring life, eh, Laurel?" I said to my two-year-old toddler who was currently running circles around the kitchen table with a yoghurt in her hand. It was flying everywhere while she screeched. I didn't have the heart to stop her. Her face was lit up, eyes bright, and a toothy smile. She was loving life, flying yoghurt and all. I waited until she'd finished her fun and then approached her.

"Right, let's get you cleaned up and then we'll go and see what Daddy's doing. No doubt having a sneaky nap, right?"

My husband Rob worked full-time as a school counsellor, although he was currently enjoying the six-week holidays. I worked from Monday to Wednesday at a local supermarket. On those days Laurel was looked after by my parents who were retired when Rob was working. I was glad it was the summer break as lately Rob had seemed fed up, and although he could be lazy, he'd been more tired than usual. I'd wondered if something at work was getting to him. He'd always said he was able to leave his work at work, but maybe one of the pupils was having an especially bad time of things. Though on holiday he'd still seemed pre-occupied. No doubt I'd have to have one of my 'talks' with him, make him say what was wrong. I knew he hated it when I got on at him, but it got things sorted. I couldn't help him with what I didn't know.

After cleaning up Laurel, she became entranced with a kids TV show so I left her to go wake Rob.

I climbed the stairs, thinking that it would be good if just for once, he asked if there was anything he could do to help at dinnertime, rather than just waiting for his evening meal to appear. Like playing with Laurel for instance so I didn't have to keep one eye on her at all times or have her 'helping'. Pushing open the door, I found he was asleep on the bed, his back to me.

"Rob, what do you want for dinner?" I asked him.

There was no response. For God's sake. It was bad enough I had to wake the toddler up and put her to bed. I didn't need a giant kid to go along with it. I jumped on the bed at the side of him and pushed him. "Rob."

Nothing.

I pushed him a few more times.

Nothing.

Jesus, how asleep was he? My mouth pinched in annoyance. I pulled him again, this time onto his back to face me. I gasped, my head jerking back as I saw Rob's face. His eyes were open; open but not awake. His expression vacant. Shaking my head, hearing my voice going, "No, no, no," I felt at his neck, but I couldn't find a pulse. There was nothing.

My own heart raced, my skin prickled, a sudden coldness hitting my stomach.

"Rob. Wake up. Wake up please. No, no, no, no. NO."

I didn't know CPR. God damn it, I knew I should have learned it, but I hadn't. I ran down the stairs, my thoughts of nothing but getting help. I grabbed my phone and dialled 999 while I opened the door and stepped outside. A delayed scream of terror left my body as the reality of what was happening hit me like an out of control juggernaut.

"Operator, which service do you require?"

"Ambulance, Hurry please." I was desperate. I couldn't wait.

"Putting you through."

By this time Violet and Milo were here. Milo stood beside me as Violet dashed past me into the house telling me she'd get Laurel.

Laurel.

My daughter was still inside the house.

I'd forgotten about my two-year-old daughter.

I told them my husband might be dead. Then I gave my address and told them exactly how I'd found him.

"An emergency ambulance has been dispatched. Stay with your husband and leave your front door open for them," I was instructed.

Ending the call, I ran back into the house, upstairs to Rob. Milo followed me. I turned to him as he came up the stairs behind me.

"Milo, it's okay. You don't have to see this. Just look after Laurel." My voice was monotone. I felt numb. Like this was happening to someone else. I was in a dream and at any moment I would wake up.

He shook his head. "Vi has Laurel, I have you. That's how this is going, Becca. Now come on."

I nodded and went back into my bedroom.

Back to Rob who was in the same place I'd left him, reaffirming to me what I did not want to believe. Any minute now he would blink his eyes and yell out that it was a trick. A joke. Any moment now. Frustrated, I got on the bed and began shaking his shoulders.

"Come on, Rob. This isn't funny anymore. Wake up." I yelled. Milo grabbed my shoulders and I snapped at him. "Get off me. I need to get him to wake up."

He firmly lifted me away and off of the bed as I fought him every step. "Becca, listen to me. You need to wait for the ambulance. You need to stand here with me and just wait, okay, just wait."

I gave up, my body still as a statue, as I waited for the ambulance to come and revive my husband, or tell me I was an idiot and his pulse was there all along. Wake him up and then I could leave this nightmare I stood in.

The ambulance people arrived and I was moved further away from the bed. I stood beside Milo, watching as they did their checks on my husband and then they called time of death. They told me they were sorry. But I was only partly aware of it as Milo's arms enfolded me and I screamed and screamed and screamed.

CHAPTER TWO

Callum

Watching my brother looking all loved up made me feel all kinds of emotions. Kinds of fucking-me-up-inside emotions. Milo was the brother I was closest to and although he would only be living over the garden, he was infatuated with Violet and I felt ecstatic for him. But it reminded me of my own sad romantic situation.

I was single and given what I'd discovered about myself, I couldn't see it was fair to have a serious relationship with anyone. Not without disclosing the truth first.

The truth I carried around inside me like a

heavy stone. The truth that only Tali and Milo knew.

That I was infertile. Couldn't have children.

It had led to me jilting my fiancée two years ago. She thought I'd just decided I didn't love her enough, but the truth was I'd loved her too much. Too much to let her marry me and not have the children she'd so dearly talked about wanting. Biological children looking like her and me. Well now she was getting married, a date set once more. Different groom. Different Daddy. Her potential future kids a mix of their mum and dad, just like she'd always wanted.

I knew we could have fostered or adopted, but I also knew Tali, inside and out, and that wouldn't have been enough for her. If we'd gone through with the wedding, Tali would have resented me eventually. I'd overheard her say to her friend that she wanted her own kids, that the thoughts of adopting worried her. Tali had always been a golden girl, a success story, and not being able to have biological children would have eaten at her. Now she'd met a golden boy and could try for happy, perfect kids.

Maybe one day I'd meet someone who didn't want any, or for whom it wasn't the be-all-and-end-all. Or maybe I'd just stay on my own and be the best uncle in the world to my brothers or sister's kids. If they ever settled down and had any.

Milo was the first one of us to settle down after my romantic failure. Not surprising given our family history. The latest news of which I was trying to get my own head around. Not forty-eight hours ago I had been introduced to my new half-brother. New in that despite the fact he was fourteen years old, none of us had known of Eli's existence.

Our mum had left us years ago and run away with Violet's uncle. Eli was the product of that relationship, which had ended as soon as she'd given birth and once again abandoned a kid. Only whereas we'd been left with a loving father who'd do anything for us, Eli had been left with a drug addict dad. Thankfully, his stepmum Angela had been around from him being a baby, to try where his father had failed. Violet had found Eli on social media and we'd met him Tuesday evening. It was now Thursday afternoon and while I fitted a new set of electrics to a block of new builds I was working on, thoughts of everything were whirling around my head like a cranial tornado. Milo settling down and Eli turning up, along with the recent news of Tali's engagement were fucking with my mind.

I'd been okay before all this. I'd got used to the single life. Thrown myself into my work. Went to the gym in an evening. Met up with friends for drinks on a Friday and Saturday night. Occasionally hooked up. Routine. Safe. Structured. A no-brainer life. Now things were being upheaved, like Milo moving out and our father telling us that Silas would be decorating the room for in case Eli wanted to stay.

God only knew what was going through my dad's mind. Having a fourteen-year-old to stay who biologically is nothing to do with you, yet a sibling to your six kids. Our mum knew how to keep the shocks coming. Now we were all wondering if there were any more stray, abandoned half-siblings out there.

After I'd found out Tali was getting married, my mind kept ruminating about whether or not I should finally tell her the reason I jilted her. Give her some closure as she moved on, because surely she'd be dreading lightening striking twice? Once jilted, I couldn't see you not worrying that it might happen again. I'd wanted her to hate me so that she didn't attempt to try to get us back together, but now she'd found someone else maybe we could have the talk I'd wanted to have all along.

My confession.

Or did part of me not want her to move on? Because she'd been mine.

Finishing up work, I popped around to the off licence and grabbed some booze to drop around to Milo's new place to congratulate him on his new address. That's if he'd answer the door because I'd expect Milo intended to christen every room of that house. He couldn't keep his hands off his girl. I refused to acknowledge the little twang that happened in my chest and gut when I thought of other people's happy ever afters. Milo would be getting married. I'd expect to be told I was best man. At least it was one wedding I'd be sure to turn up for. Unlike my own.

I pulled up outside our house, but as I went inside, weirdly there was no one home. I rolled my eyes at myself. Of course they weren't. They'd be helping Milo move in. Grabbing a quick mug full of water and tipping it down my throat, I got showered and changed and then made my way through the back gate towards Violet and Milo's.

Rocky, Vi and Milo's Staffy rescue dog, came bounding over, wagging his stumpy tail and licking my hand. "Hey, boy. You getting lots of visitors today?"

I walked into the house where I found only Finn sitting down on the sofa in the living room. "Where is everyone?" My brow furrowed as I took in Finn's expression. Troubled.

"What the fuck is going on? Is everyone alright. Is it Dad?"

He jumped up. "No, no. It's not us. It's next door. He pointed in the direction of the house attached to this one. "Becca's husband died."

"What?" My jaw dropped. "How?"

Finn shrugged. "They don't know yet. She found him in their bed, dead. Milo and Vi went running around to help but no one could do anything. They're with her and Laurel now. Dad and Juliet are there too. I said I'd stay here. An excuse so I could feel useful because I don't know how you help someone in a situation like this, Cal. I just don't."

My heart went out to the little family next door. Rob could only have been in his late twenties. Becca was too young to be a widow. Plus, their poor little girl.

My mind went back in time to around six years ago. Before Tali. To a busy Indian restaurant in

Willowfield where I'd called for a takeaway one night.

I stood near the inside doorway, tapping my foot. Happy Spice had the most amazing food, but service was always slow. Busy and popular meant waiting.

"Excuse me." I heard a small female voice come from behind me, where she'd just come through the door. "You're not called Rob, are you?"

"No, sorry. Callum." I said, not knowing why I'd decided to give her my name. I wasn't Rob, that's all she needed to know.

She nodded and took a deep breath, seemingly nervous.

"Oh, are you on a blind date?" I asked.

Her eyes widened. "Sssh."

I looked around and smiled. "No one heard me. The staff should be along shortly. They're just busy. I'm waiting for a takeaway."

"Well if my date doesn't turn up, I might be joining you." She said.

I looked her over while trying not to make it obvious. Dark, smooth skin; curly hair; dark brown eyes. She had an athletic build and a great pair of tits. She was fucking gorgeous and if this guy didn't turn up, he didn't know what he was missing. She looked around my age, maybe a couple of years older. I might chat her up just in case.

"Tell you what. If yours doesn't turn up, I'll eat my takeaway here and you can order what you want so you don't look like you've been stood up. So like I said I'm Callum and you are?"

"Rebecca."

"Hi, Rebecca."

"Hi." She smiled showing her gorgeous pearly white smile. I prayed this douchebag didn't show up.

But of course the door opened and in he came. I watched as her eyes lit up.

"Rebecca?"

"Yes." She smiled tentatively.

"I am so terribly sorry I'm late. There was an accident and I got out to help."

"Oh my goodness."

The waiter came out holding my food. "Sorry for your wait, sir."

"That's okay."

He turned to Rebecca and her blind date. "Are you booked in?"

"Yes, table for two under Staveley." The man said.

Rebecca looked at me, "Enjoy your takeaway."

"Enjoy your date." I replied, but I'd lost her. She was into her date. It was obvious.

The guy put his hand in the small of her back and off they went to their seat.

I left and ate my takeaway.

I didn't think about her again. Had no idea she'd been living on the Smalldale estate until Violet moved in a month ago and made friends with her. It had been a shock, finding out she lived so near, that she'd married her blind date and had a kid. I'd been happy for her. There'd been no *Milo Waite, 'I'd seen the woman of my dreams and had to make her mine'* thoughts. We'd just been a moment in time in a takeaway, where we could have ended up spending time together. I'd been eighteen; I'd moved straight along.

Until I'd seen her chatting and laughing with Violet. And then my mind had started wondering about *what if Rob hadn't turned up that night? Would anything have happened?*

"Earth calling Cal."

I startled, having been completely lost in thought. "Sorry, I'm just so fucking shocked."

"I feel you, bro. There's not really anything we can do though is there?"

"No." I replied sadly. I took a seat on the sofa at the side of Finn. "I'll keep you company in looking after Rocky."

It was a couple of hours later when Violet, Milo, Juliet, and Dad came back. Violet's eyes were puffy and red. Everyone else looked shellshocked. Rocky offered everyone a lick and a fuss which brought a smile to the harried looking faces.

"I just can't believe it." Violet said.

"Do they know how he died?" I asked.

She shook her head. "There's got to be a post-mortem. Becca's parents have insisted on taking her and Laurel back to theirs, but it was a struggle to get her to leave. How will she ever be happy in that house again though? Every time she goes in that room, she's going to remember what happened today."

We all took it as a rhetorical question. All I knew was that I wished I could do something to help Becca.

But I couldn't. Because I was no one to her, no one at all.

CHAPTER THREE

Becca

It had been a week since Rob died. A week where to some extent I'd died myself, inside. Numb was my new middle name. My mum said it was a normal part of grief. Part of denial.

Today was his funeral. I was back in my house, sitting in my living room, dressed in black. I'd always felt funerals weren't a place for children, but there was no way I was leaving Laurel with anyone else. I needed her close to me. The part of Rob I still had. She looked more like me, but she had Rob's upturned nose and every so often she'd fix me with a look that was all him.

I'd fallen instantly in love with Rob as soon as

we'd met at a blind date at an Indian restaurant set up by my college friend. Rob was her cousin who'd seen a photo of me with her and begged her to set it up. He'd kept me waiting for ten minutes. I'd thought I was being stood up, but then he'd walked through the door and my heart had leapt as he'd apologised and smiled at me. I'd never forget his hand in the small of my back as he took me towards our seats. I'd felt a frisson of excitement that it might lead to his hand on my naked body at some point.

It had led to so much more. Two years of dating, four years of marriage, and a beautiful two-year-old daughter.

And now he was gone and there was a void where my heart had beat for him. The post-mortem had revealed an aneurism. A ticking time bomb in his brain that went off. Nothing anyone could have done.

I looked across at Rob's mother. She only had Rob. She'd never really been a maternal type and had rarely seen Laurel, yet now she kept talking to me about not losing touch and regular visits to our daughter. I went through the motions, nodding, agreeing, when I wanted to ask where she'd been for the majority of the last two years. But I didn't.

Because I would be dignified, dressed in my smart black dress, with my smart black shoes, while people offered their condolences. I would accept them while not fully acknowledging what they said. Sorry for my loss? What loss?

Deny.

Deny.

Deny.

There would be more of this to endure after the service. When staff from Rob's school and extended family and friends gathered at his graveside. No cremation for my husband. We'd briefly talked about our burial arrangements when I was pregnant with Laurel, when we'd got all serious and planned our wills. He'd said he wanted somewhere for our future child to visit, if they wanted to. He wanted that option for them. So there would be a service and then there would be a burial.

"The cars have arrived." My mum stood beside me at one side, Violet at the other, while my dad fussed to make sure the door got locked. There was nothing a burglar could take from me. My whole life was in my arms, and in the coffin in the back of the hearse outside my door. As I left my house, people stood on the street. They'd left their houses to stand with heads bowed as we made our way to the local church. People who had possibly never spoken to us in our lives, today felt the need to let me know they were thinking about us and it meant more than they could ever know. I climbed into the family car. Me and Laurel; Mum and Dad; and Rob's mum, Paula.

They chattered on, conversing with my daughter's babble while I stared out of the window watching the expressions of people in the streets as the hearse passed them. Bowed heads, shock, avoidance and quickly turned away heads, indifference to the fact my world had been torn apart. It was all there outside my neighbourhood. Life continuing.

I sat through the service numb while a vicar who'd never met my husband spoke about him. They played hymns that we'd had at our wedding, and I'd chosen the often used Angels by Robbie Williams as the song to play us out.

And then I stood at a graveside on a warm August day and watched them lower Rob's coffin into the ground.

It hit me at that point. Rob was in there. My husband was in there. He was dead. I would never see him again. I quickly passed Laurel's hand into my mother's just before my legs gave way. I rubbed the heel of my palm against my chest, because I was sure my heart was shattering. No longer an empty space. I was full of pain. Tears poured down my face and I felt like I couldn't breathe. My father's arms came around me and I heard him.

"My poor baby girl." He kissed the top of my head. "It'll be okay. It'll be okay." He promised.

The one thing I would remember about the funeral. The thing that stood out as I was leaving to get back in the funeral car. I saw that a few teenagers stood alongside a teacher I recognised from Rob's school. Two teenage boys and one girl looked at me. The teacher mouthed he was sorry, one boy smiled at me, the other looked away. The girl's eyes poured with tears. Rob had supported these children. Now they would have to confide in someone new. I felt so sorry for them because they already had difficulties and now they'd suffered the loss of the person supporting them.

From the graveside we travelled to a pub where I'd arranged for a small buffet. I gathered myself together ready to accept more condolences.

"It'll all be over soon, love, and then we'll get you back to ours and you can have a nice bath."

"I want to go back home." I told my mum. "It's time. I need to accept what's happened."

"Let's talk about it later." She said. I knew I wouldn't get my way. Not tonight at least.

I excused myself to visit the bathroom. Violet approached me on my way there. We might have only been in the early stages of friendship, but something had clicked and I liked her a lot. The fact she lived next door would help me I knew when I eventually returned home.

"You need me for anything?"

I shook my head. "No, but thanks. I'm just off to visit the ladies."

"I'll come with you."

"I'm perfectly capable of having a wee by myself." I smiled. The first smile I'd had in a long time. Turned out it would be the last smile I'd have for a long time too.

As I waited for the bathroom, the teenage girl from earlier appeared. "Mrs Staveley. Could I speak with you? In private?" I rolled my eyes at Violet. "Sure, honey." I stood just outside the bathroom door, hoping she'd hurry up with her condolences so I wouldn't wet myself.

"I've tried to come see you at your house, but you weren't there."

I frowned. For one thing who'd told her where we lived? "I've been staying with my parents."

She started to cry again.

"I loved him." She said, her chin wobbling. Oh bless, a schoolgirl crush. It did happen from time to time; they saw Rob as a knight in shining armour because he'd offer them hope.

I put my arms around her. "Oh, honey. We all did... do."

She pushed me away and this time her eyes were harder and her chin tilted up. "You don't understand. I loved him and he loved me."

I laughed. I couldn't help it. "Don't be ridiculous."

She placed a hand on her stomach. "And I'm having his baby." She said.

I didn't have time for this nonsense. I'd just buried my husband. "Where the fuck is your teacher?" I shouted. Violet came to my side.

"What's going on?"

"What's going on is while I'm trying to get through my day, this kid is telling me she's having my husband's baby. I need her teacher because I know the children he saw had problems but this is ridiculous. I don't need this today of all days."

Violet grabbed the girl's arm. "Let's go."

She shrugged her off. Her chin jutting out some more. "Take your hands off me. I'm not lying." She whipped back around to me. "I was sleeping with him. I'm having his child."

"Get out." I screeched, and now we were attracting an audience. My mum came dashing through the door, no doubt alerted by someone from the bathroom queue.

I was done. "The wake is over. Everyone needs to leave." I continued shouting, as my mum put her arm around me. Violet followed the girl out of the room. She looked over her shoulder at me. "I'll get Milo to tell people to go home. And I'll go and talk to this teacher."

"You can talk all you want." The girl raised her voice. "It won't change anything about the baby in my belly."

"Get me out of here." I told my mother.

"There's a back exit. Come on, I'll get your father to meet us in the car park." She took her mobile phone from her bag and dialled while I followed her. We were almost at the door when a male voice stopped me.

"Mrs Staveley? Could I just have a quick word?"

The man's hands were shaking, I noted. He didn't want to have a conversation with me really, not today, but his job meant he had to. It wasn't his fault that one of his pupils was a fantasist with a crush.

"Just give me one minute, Mum." I told her and I took a step forward, nodding at the man. I couldn't remember his name; all introductions and condolences had swum into one long river of grief.

"I am so, so sorry to have to talk to you about this today of all days. This is the first I've heard about all this. If I'd had any inclination, I obviously wouldn't have brought Zoey here today."

"It's fine. But... she said she'd been to my house. Can you have a word with her parents? Make sure she doesn't do that again. And get her another counsellor. There must be someone who works across the school holidays? She's obviously seriously troubled."

The teacher cleared his throat and pulled slightly at his shirt collar and then at his tie. "After I drop them back home, I'll phone the Head, but if Zoey continues to make this accusation then there will have to be an investigation, school holidays or not."

"For God's sake. Does she not realise a man just died? That I'm in mourning? I don't need my time wasting by some stupid teenager who's making crap up."

Then Zoey appeared again, one of the boys trying to hold her back. "I'm sorry, Mr Timmins. I told her not to come back."

"I'm not lying. Get it into your head. We'd been sleeping together from my sixteenth birthday. For six months. I'm having his baby. We were in love."

"Enough." My mother yelled. "We're leaving. Do whatever investigations you need to do and leave my daughter the hell alone." She raged at Zoey. "My baby just lost her husband. Have you no shame?"

"I lost him too." She yelled back.

Paula had been at the back listening. She stepped toward Zoey.

"What if she's telling the truth?" She said to my mum.

"Don't be ridiculous." My mother snapped, her eyes scornful.

Paula stepped to the side of Zoey. "Then you'd be shouting at a young girl who's carrying my grandchild. Another piece of my son."

"You hardly bother with Laurel so that's rich." My mother had clearly had enough of biting her tongue. "We're going, Becca. Your father is waiting." She basically pushed me out of the door.

Once in the car I listened as my mum explained everything to my dad, but all I could think was that Rob hadn't touched me for approximately six months.

What if Zoey wasn't lying?

CHAPTER FOUR

Callum

I finished work earlier than usual because my mind wasn't on the job. It was thinking about poor Becca. Today was the funeral. Milo and Vi were going. The rest of us just sent a wreath from the family and made a donation to the brain tumour charity she'd chosen.

I made a brew and sat down in the kitchen waiting for the others to get home. My phone pinged.

Eli:Do you think Ezra would show me around a film set or take me to a premiere?

I laughed to myself. Looked like my little brother was thinking of all the important things to do with his siblings. And then I stopped short. Had anyone actually told Ezra about Eli?

I hadn't.

No one did the night we met him.

Fuck, he might not know.

I realised I needed to check with the others and then if not, I'd call him and give him the news; before Eli turned up in the US and demanded to meet the A-list.

I sent him a message back.

Cal:Steady on, E. Give us a chance to get to know you before you try and bugger off to Hollywood!

Eli:Okay, lol. Bro.

Cal:It's weird isn't it? You look so much like Silas and Finn.

Eli:I know. When can I come over again?

Cal:I'll ask at teatime tonight and text you. Only Vi's neighbour's husband died so it's been a bit weird around here and busy.

Eli:Oh no. Okay, let me know. I can't wait.

Cal:Actually, fancy going bowling Saturday night? If it's okay with Angela, that is? I don't know if any of the others will come, but I could do with getting out of here.

There's a short wait before my phone pings.

Eli:Angela says it's okay but she'll come too. Which place and what time?

Cal:About six? We can have a meal there. Texting you other details now.

I added a link to the bowling alley.

Eli:Cool. See you then, Bro.

I smiled as I put my phone back on the table. At least I could put my spare time to good use at the moment by getting to know Eli and make his getting used to us all a little easier. Because we only had to get to know *him*, whereas he had six siblings and Josh Waite to get used to.

The door banged and after hearing shoes being kicked off, Silas walked into the kitchen. My older brother looked flushed in the face. Trouble was, you never knew if it was because of his fitness instructor job or due to a shagathon. Sometimes I reckoned he combined the two. He went straight to the fridge, took out the opened carton of orange juice and drank the whole thing down before throwing the carton on the side.

"Bin."

"I'd have to walk over to do that. I'm knackered, mate."

"I meant you. Human garbage disposal."

He tapped his vest top at his abdomen. "Got to keep my stamina up. I'm in demand."

"Please don't tell me anymore. It's been too long."

"I can set you up?"

"No." I blurted out. "Absolutely not. I can arrange my own hook-ups."

Silas shrugged. "Well let me know, cos I get offered that much I have to turn some of it down. And it's not good for business."

I frowned. "You should keep those two sides separate. Business and pleasure. You're going to come unstuck."

"Okay, Mom."

I flinched.

"Fuck, you know what I mean."

"Yeah, I know. Hey, did you tell Ezra?"

"Nope. Ha, did no one tell him yet?"

"Not sure."

"Well he took himself away, out of sight. Made it clear he didn't want to be here, so he can't blame us if we forget he exists from time to time. I'm off for a shower."

"I'm taking Eli bowling Saturday night. Want to come?"

"Yeah, why not?"

"Okay, be at Bowled Over at around six."

"Got it. Six. Kick your arses at bowling."

"In your dreams." I shouted after him.

As I went to pick up the carton to put it in the bin, I saw Vi outside watering the plants. They were back then. I headed out to ask how everything had gone.

"Hey, Violet." I kept to my side of the gate as Rocky was running around. As soon as he heard me, he ran over jumping up.

"Rocky, get down." Violet told him off but stroked him a million times at the same time.

"Just thought I'd ask how it went."

Violet's lips pursed. "Not good. Not good at all."

"Fuck. She not handling it well? I'm not surprised with the suddenness of it."

"It wasn't that. To be honest she held herself together quite well, apart from a moment at the burial. It was the little performance that came after. One of Rob's pupils; you know he did counselling at school?"

I didn't. I had no clue about anything to do with Becca's husband, but I nodded so she'd continue.

"Well, one of them told Becca she was pregnant with Rob's baby."

"What?"

"I know. Right in the middle of the wake. And the best of it is, the teacher told Becca they'd have to look into it. As if it's true. I know the kid might have problems but that was really low."

"But what if it is true?" I asked Violet.

She tilted her head downwards and raised her brows, like I was suggesting the moon really was made of cheese.

"Don't be crazy. She was like sixteen."

"And?"

"Cal." She sighed. "It's been a heavy day. Can

we not do this now? I've come out to water the plants because I've got a bit of a headache starting."

"I'm sorry. It wasn't meant to wind you up. But listen, just... I don't know... keep a corner of your mind on what if it is true. Just that tiny bit. Because if it is, Becca will need you more than ever."

She took a deep breath and looked up for a moment before her eyes came back to mine. "I hope to fucking God it's not true, because she's got to be at rock bottom right now as it is."

"It's probably a crock of shit. Like you said the kids he worked with would have been complex. Kid was probably attention seeking as a reaction to her own loss, but Milo said Becca doesn't really have a best mate or anything. She's going to need you and Juliet."

"I've not known you for long, Callum Waite, but I seem to be getting the impression that you're the one who makes sure everyone is okay. The protector. You're stepping up with Eli, who has already told me how excited he is about bowling; and you're looking out for the neighbour you barely know. Who looks out for you, Callum Waite?"

She put her hand on top of mine on the gate and squeezed. "Don't forget to look out for yourself okay?"

I didn't get to reply because my brother came charging out of the house. "What are you doing molesting my brother, Princess? Is one Waite brother not enough for you?"

"You coming bowling Saturday night, Miley?" I asked him.

"Sure thing. And I'll bring, Vi, so she can see me bending and showing off my pert butt."

I saw when his thoughts reached a different conclusion. "You're not playing, Princess." He told her. "I'm not having anyone but me checking out that arse."

"There's only one arse around here that people are noticing." Violet quipped. "I'll see you Saturday, Cal. And remember, my door is always open."

I nodded.

"It's our door, not your door, and it's not always open, at some times it is most definitely locked." Milo picked her up and put her over his shoulder. Then as he realised her backside would be facing me, he began to walk backwards. "Bowling. Text me the deets." He shouted and then checking behind himself he went into the house, closed the door with a wink on his face, and I heard the lock turn.

Before I went back into our house, I looked up

at Becca's top windows. The curtains remained drawn. I wondered if she'd ever actually come back to live there. I shouldn't imagine she'd want to stay in the place where her husband died.

Anyway, it wasn't my problem. But it was my night to fix dinner, so I went inside to make a start on prep and then if no one else had done it, tonight I'd call Ezra.

Sure enough, I discovered that no one had thought to tell Ezra. Not even Dad, who looked particularly guilty. I clapped him on the back. "Dad, I think you can forgive yourself. It's all been a bit full on lately."

"Yes, it's certainly been that. I'd better call him and catch him up with things." He scratched at his chin. Dad and Ezra's relationship had become strained over the years. I think Dad felt Ezra blamed him for Mum leaving. I didn't know if there was any truth in it. Ezra always maintained he just followed his dreams.

I went up to my room and closed the door. This room had been Ezra's before it had been mine. I'd shared with Milo, which I think is why I was closer to him than the others. I'd had to bunk up when

Juliet was born. Once Ezra left, I'd thankfully been able to move out. My room was on the small side, but it was all I needed. I wasn't one for having lots of stuff. It looked out over the front of the house. If it had been at the back maybe I'd have known Becca lived so close sooner.

I pressed FaceTime and after a few rings, my elder brother answered.

"Videocall. Must be a crisis. Let me guess, Silas got someone up the duff?"

"Nope. He's still a horndog, but no strays as far as we know."

But a stray is what I'm calling about.

"So?" He raised his eyebrows. Straight to the point as ever. I looked over his features because I'd not seen him for a long time. His blonde hair was slightly grown out, his blue eyes the only thing he had in common with me. All of the Waites had various shades of brown hair, but Ezra's was light blonde, like our paternal grandfather's. He'd always had to be different.

It was rare to find him looking like the brother I remembered. Usually he'd taken on the persona of the character he was playing. He could have different coloured hair, be slimmer, be fatter. Ezra was a chameleon.

"I'll just come out with it as quickly as possible because I really don't know how to say it, but we have a half-brother. He's fourteen. Mum had a kid with Dan Dawson and abandoned him the minute he was born."

Ezra's face mottled as I watched. His neck corded and his nostrils flared. "She fucking did what? Are you kidding me right now?"

I shook my head. "I wish I was, Ezra, but I'm not. And Dan died, drug overdose. The kid's largely been raised by a stepmum."

I explained how Violet had looked up Dan on Facebook, finding out he'd died but that Elias existed, and she'd got in touch. Ezra knew Violet was Marg Dawson's grandaughter, but he'd not realised how fast Milo had worked his magic on her, so I told him about Milo moving in with Violet.

As I continued to speak, I saw him calm down.

"Bloody hell. She must really love him to put up with his ways. I'm surprised he asked her to marry him and didn't just tell her."

"I'm sure if she'd said no, he would have."

That made Ezra smile. A rare sight. I don't remember the last time I saw it.

"So you've met this kid, our newfound brother?"

"Yeah, and I'm taking him bowling this weekend. He seems a good kid, though his stepmum told Dad not to be fooled by the innocent act and said he could be a devil."

"Well that can't be a surprise given his heritage. Fuck, another brother. Bet Juliet's pissed it's a boy."

"She's just pleased it means she's not the youngest anymore. She wants us to pick on Eli now instead."

"Never gonna happen. She's the only girl. Even I still give her shit from over here."

"You do?" I wasn't aware Ezra was in touch with anyone regularly.

"Yeah, not very often, but I still do it."

"So, anyway, your new brother wants to know if you can get him a straight pass to the red carpet to meet as many other stars as possible." I winked.

"Kids. Well as it happens, I have a new film coming out with a London premiere. It's not for months yet but maybe I could take him along. Don't tell him though. I don't want to get his hopes up if I can't do it."

"You might be coming to the UK?"

"Mayyybbe."

"Will you visit?"

A slow smile spread across his face. "I guess I need to come meet my new half-brother and do my bit for family relations, but I doubt I'll stay long. You know me. The whole Waite family thing suffocates me. I need my space."

"I know." I paused for a moment, chewing on my bottom lip. "Do you think she had any more?"

"What?"

"Mum. Do you think she might have done it again? That there could be another abandoned kid or two somewhere."

"Who the fuck knows? She's certainly got some questions to answer."

"Huh, yeah. Except no one knows where she is to answer them. What if she's dead too? Like Dan."

"I don't want to talk about her anymore. It pisses me off. Send me a photo of the kid and his telephone number. I guess I ought to introduce myself to him at some point."

"He'll fucking wet himself with excitement."

"He'll soon realise I'm the least exciting Waite of them all."

I sighed. "That's not true and you know it."

I heard a door open and a female voice.

"I've got to go." He said and ended the FaceTime.

I wondered if he'd settled down yet, found someone? There were plenty of photos of him with women online if you looked him up, but there'd never been anything you'd call long term. I hoped he did come home soon. I missed him.

CHAPTER FIVE

Becca

I stepped into my mum and dad's house and told them I was going to get myself and Laurel changed. I needed out of the black formal clothes. I put Laurel a t-shirt and shorts on and I dressed in my pyjamas and added a robe.

"Daddy home soon?" Laurel said, her big brown eyes staring up at me. She held her fairy doll, Luna, tight under her arm.

"Oh, sweetie." I picked her up and placed her on my knee. "Do you remember what I told you?" I stroked my hand through her dark curls. "The angels took Daddy up to heaven. He got very, very ill."

"I want Daddy."

Her bottom lip wobbled and I hugged her closer to me, inhaling the sweet smell that was all my baby girl. "Me too, Laurel. Me too."

I stroked her back. She curled up into me and before long, soft little breaths came from her as she fell asleep. It had been a big day for her. Long and overwhelming with all the people fussing around her. She was off her usual routine but who cared. For now, she could sleep. Escape the reality of life without her darling daddy.

I carried her to the double bed we had been sharing and put her under the covers, tucking her in with Luna and with Hugo, the toy dog Rob had bought her when she was one and had just learned to walk. She loved both of them, but Hugo suffered the most as she liked to twiddle and suck on his ears which had now had to be repaired several times. Lying at the side of her for a moment, I wondered what we were meant to do now. Our future, the one I'd thought we'd have with Rob, was gone. Every day I woke up having forgotten and then like Groundhog Day, I'd remember and the pain would hit all over again. Fresh new waves daily. I couldn't stay here at my parents' house much longer. I needed to try to get Laurel back to her usual routines.

I came to the decision that tomorrow I was going back home. I needed to go through Rob's things. I needed to sort out paperwork. It would keep me busy.

You need to see if there's anything about Zoey. The thought was unwelcome. But they kept coming. Ever since she'd made her stupid announcement at the funeral. Yes, she was a teenager with problems; yes, it was probably all lies; but while I was trying to mourn the loss of my husband, she was like a slow spreading poison.

What if it's true?

What if he fucked her?

What if he got her pregnant?

What if the last months of your marriage were a sham?

And if it's true, is it the first time, or has he been deceiving you all along?

And I hated her for it. More than she could ever know, because Rob was my darling, beloved husband. Just over a week ago we had taken Laurel to a local farm and we'd smiled at each other and held hands as we watched her face beam with delight, together. Shared the looks we knew the words for without speaking. Were wrapped in a happy bubble of love and joy.

And now I was doubting his memory. Just the tiniest bit. Not consciously, but just by that tormenting inner voice.

What if he did it?

Leaving Laurel curled up looking oh-so-content in sleep with a peace I wasn't sure I'd ever feel again, I pulled my robe tighter around myself and made my way downstairs. My mother shot my father a look as I passed.

"I'd not realised it was bedtime." She said. "I thought it was four in the afternoon."

"Leave her, Esther." Dad stuck up for me. I went into the kitchen, opened the fridge and took out a bottle of apple juice, pouring myself a large glass. I felt like I needed vitamins. The thought flashed in my mind that now Laurel only had one parent, I must keep healthy.

"I'm moving back home tomorrow." I announced to my parents.

They both began to protest. I let them have their say and then I sat down on the chair opposite the sofa.

"Look. I know I have a room here. I know I can come back here at any point I feel I can't cope. You two have been amazing. I couldn't ask for better parents. But I want to go home. It will help me to accept that he's gone. Will help Laurel realise he's not coming home."

A tear ran down my mum's cheek. "I wish this had not happened to you, sweetheart. You shouldn't have had to bury your husband today. It's not like he'd had a decent innings like your dad."

My dad snorted in disgust. "Are you saying I should be dead instead? You wish. You'd spend all my bloody money on more bloody clothes. I'm only sixty-two, woman."

Their banter made me laugh. It was just so normal within these days of the abnormal. Dad grinned at me, clearly delighted that he'd brought a smile to my face. "You know there's a place for you here, any time, day or night. You just either ring me to fetch you or you call a cab if you need to and get here. I have money in the house ready to pay for it. You understand?"

I nodded my head at him. "I understand. Right, what's on the television?"

We all pretended for a while that everything was okay, even though it was far from it.

. . .

The next morning, despite my mother asking me if I was sure for what seemed like a million times, my dad drove me back to Redwood Road. Despite wanting to hang around, there wasn't really anywhere for him to park which suited me fine. I reassured him that I'd be okay and that I'd rather be alone. Well, alone with Laurel.

I was pleased that no one seemed to see me enter the house. Just for a while, I wanted to spend time with Laurel, on our own, while I got reacquainted with the house that used to be our home, our happy ever after.

As I opened the door, I had to give it a decent shove. Post was piled up on the floor at the other side of the door. Envelopes with handwriting were apparent. Sympathy cards. I gently kicked them out of the way while I got Laurel inside.

"Wait there for Mummy a minute while I bring our bags in, sweetie. You stand by the window." I got the bags off the doorstep and left them in the hallway at the side of the stairs. Gathering the mail, I brought it into the living room and threw it down on the coffee table for the time being. Walking over to Laurel and crouching down, I removed her little summer cardigan, and then her shoes, replacing those with her slippers.

"Do you want a drink?"

"Please. Squash. Daddy not home?"

My confused little baby. I picked her up and looked up at her. "No, my darling. Daddy died, remember? He's in heaven. We can talk to him in the sky and he'll hear us."

Her little face crumpled up in confusion. As I walked into the kitchen with her, she announced, "Biscuit?" and just like that she'd moved on. If only I could do the same.

Once she'd had her drink and biscuit, I put the children's TV channel on to keep her occupied while I went around the house opening curtains and windows to let the light and fresh air in. It would only be a matter of time before Violet noticed and so I sent her a text telling her I was home, but I wanted to be alone for the day. She messaged back that she totally understood.

The only bedroom I'd not been in was our own. I pushed open the door. Memories of finding Rob on the bed assaulted me. In a flash of fury, I began tearing off the bedding from the bed. Sweat poured off me given the heat of the day but I continued until it was all on the floor in a heap and I stood panting at the side of it. I could never sleep in this bed again. There and then I knew that I would ask Milo to dismantle it and take it away and for now I would be sleeping in my daughter's room. She had a sofa bed. They were supposed to be for occasional use, but for now that was where I would be.

After rinsing my face with cold water in the bathroom, I returned to the bedroom and opened Rob's drawer in the bottom of his wardrobe. It was where he'd kept what I'd always called his 'junk'. The odd photograph, a watch that used to belong to his dad, stray buttons, certificates. Random paperwork. I lifted out the drawer and carried it downstairs.

Of course no sooner did I do this than Laurel came nosying. I handed her the watch and she took it with her back towards the television, having realised the drawer offered no further value. I went through every item but there was nothing to indicate a secret past.

Zoey was a vicious, lying bitch who was ruining my memories and invading my time to mourn.

I wanted to throw something. My pulse sped and heartbeat pounded as I felt the fury grow inside me. Heat flushed through my body. But I couldn't let any of it go. It would frighten my daughter. Instead I walked through the kitchen, and I crawled onto my knees and let out a silent scream. My jaw felt like it was breaking with the strain.

What the fuck did I do now? I felt like I was going insane. Engulfed in grief like a strangling shroud. I needed an out. I walked through the side door of the kitchen that led past a downstairs toilet and out of the outer door where I sat on the steps gasping in fresh air.

I closed my eyes and prayed to a God I'd never really bothered with before.

What do I do?

What do I do?

What do I do?

My phone buzzed and I opened it to find a message from my mum checking on how we were doing. I sent back a 'yes, we're fine' and then huffed at the ridiculousness of it all. Staring at my phone, I had a thought. Where was Rob's?

Feeling motivated, I went back into the house, looking until I found it under the bed. It must have fallen there during everything. The battery was dead and so I plugged it into the charger in the hallway and I waited.

I got busy with Laurel and decided that I wasn't looking at it until she was in bed.

But she wouldn't go to bed. Wouldn't go to sleep. Instead she screamed for her daddy. I tried to tell her over and over and over, but a two-year-old couldn't understand death; she just knew that her daddy said goodnight to her every night and tonight he wasn't here.

She threw herself on the floor and she stamped her feet until she'd got so hot and bothered I had to get a damp cloth for her head. With no other options, I asked if she wanted to watch some television and I took her back downstairs knowing eventually exhaustion would take her over.

But as I put the light back on in the living room there was a click and all the house went dark. It was the final straw and as I walked into the living room with streetlights showing me the way, I sat down on the sofa placing Laurel next to me and I called Violet.

"I'm so sorry to disturb you. I don't know what to do. My electrics have failed. We're in the dark." My voice trembled as I spoke to my friend.

"I'd send Milo, but if it's the electrics, we may

as well see if Callum's in. He'll come straight round I'm sure. Disturb me any time, you know that. Do you want me to come around?"

"No. No. Just get Callum, please. I'd be so grateful. I just need my electricity. Things are frustrating enough." Part of me wanted her to insist that she came around. There was no suiting me right now.

"I'll call him straightaway."

"Thank you."

"Ring me tomorrow?"

"I will. I promise."

I sat back on the sofa stroking my daughter's hair and telling her that the television was broken but a man was coming around to mend it.

Footsteps sounded up the path and I made my way to the front door to let in Callum Waite. I'd only met him in passing when he'd been working in Violet's house and so it seemed strange to be letting him in at ten o'clock at night. I laughed wondering if anyone had seen the widow letting a strange man in at this hour. Brenda who served at the mini-supermarket would be in her element with such gossip.

I noticed Callum look at me weirdly. I was probably looking back at him the same way. To this virtual stranger on my path. He had similarities in his looks to Milo in that you could see they were brothers if you knew them both, but Callum was a lot slimmer and a little shorter. Where Milo held himself with confidence, there was a reticence with Callum, a gentleness. Or maybe I was reading too much into the fact he was waiting to be invited in?

"Sorry, Callum. Come in. I'm having strange thoughts. Excuse me." I stepped back to let him inside.

"It's Cal, and don't worry about it. The dark will do that to you. Makes you think of monsters and things that go bump in the night."

I looked wide-eyed in the direction of my daughter expecting a panic about the word 'monsters' but there were tiny little snores coming from the sofa. Typical.

"So I put the light on and there was a ping and then everything went off." I attempted to explain. "That's my technical term for you, a ping."

He smiled. "Okay, so I'm guessing you don't usually look at the fuse box."

"Nope. That would be... have been, Rob's domain." I told him.

"Well it's—"

"In the box near to the side door." I finished for him. "I know where it is, just not how it works."

"Yeah, so can I go through?"

"Unless you can repair it through telepathy." I said sarcastically. God, my mouth just didn't know when to quit. "I'm so sorry. Yes, of course. Let's go through." I walked through the kitchen, through the side door and pointed to the box on the wall near to the downstairs loo. He opened it and shone a torch inside where there were all these weird looking parts with switches.

"So that's the main switch." Cal shone a light on one part. "That's not been tripped. If you see here, that one is up when it should be down. It's your lighting. My guess is your bulb went and tripped the circuit. My next question is do you have a spare bulb for your living room?"

After removing the bulb and changing it for a new one, Cal flicked the switch back and all the electricity came back on.

"Oh thank God."

"Well, it was me really, but I guess the big guy created everything in the first place."

I tilted my head at him. "Thank you, Cal. I can't tell you how grateful I am that you came round tonight. I'm glad Violet moved in, or I'd never have known you were there."

He opened his mouth as if to say something, but then closed it again. I presumed it was going to be his sympathies.

"I want to ask how you're doing but I realise that's the stupidest fucking question ever, so I'm not asking it. But the thought is there." He said.

It was no good. I actually sniggered.

"Oh thank you, Cal." I began to full on laugh. It was entirely inappropriate, but I couldn't stop myself.

"Fuck, take back what I said. I am asking it. How are you doing?"

The more I looked at the pained expression on his face, as he shook his head and berated himself, the more tears began to run down my cheek. But they weren't tears of sadness. They were tears of relief, because as Callum Waite stood in front of me, he didn't know what to do either.

And that made two of us.

CHAPTER SIX

Callum

I'd been in the living room watching some car salvage programme or something equally brain numbing when I'd got a call from Violet. At first, I'd worried about Milo, but instead I'd found myself getting my tools together to go around to Becca's house.

I'd seen the curtains were open, the windows open too, but I didn't know if she had someone just looking over the place for her while she was at her parents' home. Now I'd been asked to go and help her with a power cut. What the hell did I say to her?

Turned out, I'd said the wrong thing and had

the woman standing in front of me in fits of hysterical laughter, tears rolling down her cheeks. The more awkward I felt, the more I tried to apologise, the more she laughed.

Eventually, after a few extremely awkward minutes and two attempts at stopping, Becca stood in front of me, rubbing at her eyes.

"I'm so sorry, Cal." She took some deep breaths. "Basically, I don't know how this widow shit works and I hate it. I'm trying to behave how people think I should and the fact you said you wanted to ask but thought it a bit pointless, well, that just hit the spot."

I wasn't quite sure they'd been my words, but I wasn't arguing with the woman.

"You don't know how to act with me. I don't know how to act with anyone. My head is a mess."

"That's understandable. You just lost your husband." *And he might have got someone else pregnant.*

"Yeah and with that has come information that I don't know what to do with. But you don't need to hear that."

Becca looked like a woman who wanted to talk. Wanted to but felt she couldn't. She was smacking her lips like they held an ocean of words behind them, but they threatened to drown someone if spoken.

"Becca."

"Mmm-hmmm."

"Now the leccy is working, are you going to make me a cup of tea? Seems the least you can do, and then, even though we've barely spoken before, you can say what's on your mind, and I vow to never repeat it. Use me to get whatever's eating at you off your chest."

She stood there, mulling over my words.

"Can I just put Laurel in her room?"

"Of course."

And that's how I found myself on the sofa in Becca's living room waiting for her to come downstairs and make me a drink and to confide in me about the reality of what had just happened to her. And rather than want to run for the hills, away from a newly bereaved woman and her raw emotions, instead I got up and filled the kettle myself.

I heard her footsteps pad down the stairs and so I busied myself in the kitchen getting mugs ready just so I wouldn't be staring at her when she came in.

"Are you sure you want to stay for a drink?"

"Sure. Want to tell me where the tea and coffee are kept and what you want?"

"I'm giving you an out, Cal. I know you Waite guys are good guys, but you're free to go."

I turned to her and waved the kettle. "You said I could have a drink, so I'm staying. So, tea or coffee?"

Becca walked over and opened the cupboard above my head. "In here, but I'll pass thanks. I'm going to have a whisky if you want to join me?"

"You drink whisky?"

Becca's mouth quirked at the edge. "Do you know how many times I've been asked that question? What is it about whisky that makes it unusual for a woman to want to drink it? Is it a tough drink with its smoke and peat tones? Are women not strong enough to take it?"

"You're right. It was an arse of a question. Personally, I prefer a pina colada."

Her mouth dropped open.

"Why do women do that face when I say I like a pina colada?"

"You're right. Sorry though, I don't have any."

I sniggered. "I'm messing with you. I love whisky. Yes please." I put the kettle down.

"Oh my god, you fucker." Becca pushed me in

the arm. Then she reached for two tumblers and went into the wine rack for the whisky.

"Neat, lemonade, water, or just ice?"

"How you're having it."

"Tonight, I'm drinking it neat. Fuck it. Though if I pour myself a third you have permission to take it out of my hands. I have my daughter to think about."

I followed her into the living room and took a seat. She poured us both a drink and handed mine to me, taking the other seat on the sofa. I almost raised it to hers in a cheers, enough that my hand went forward and then back again. She noticed and shoved her hand forward.

"Here's to conversations between kind-of neighbours about the fucked-upness of life." She clinked her glass into mine. "It's not strange at all to talk to a virtual stranger about how your marriage might not have been all you think, is it?" She took a large mouthful of her drink and didn't flinch. In fact, she closed her eyes, smacked her lips together and seemed to relish the burn.

I met her gaze. "We're not strangers. I have a fact for you that you haven't realised. Do you remember the night you met Rob?" I asked her, deciding to be straight with her.

"We went to an Indian." Her brow furrowed, waiting for me to elaborate.

"He was late and you conversed with a stranger in the doorway. That stranger was me."

Becca's eyes widened. "Shut the front door. How'd you remember that? I remember talking to someone but nothing else. It was years ago."

I shrugged my shoulders, not about to tell the widow that I found her unforgettable. "I've a good memory, but so, see, we're not strangers. We've known each other years."

"I think that's reaching, but I need to fucking talk to someone so I'm going along with it anyway."

Although I knew what she was about to say, I decided to keep my mouth shut and let her tell me herself. To unburden herself.

She took a deep inhale and exhale. "At the funeral, a pupil Rob worked with came up to me and announced she was carrying his baby."

I widened my eyes and waited to see if she said anything else, but there was silence for me to fill.

"And what's the evidence in either direction?"

"There's nothing. Nothing at all. Just her word. I've begun to look through his things, but there's nothing." She paused again. "Nothing so far. And I find myself in the unusual situation of mourning a husband I loved dearly, the father to my child, with a question mark about how he loved me back thanks to a stupid teenage girl who probably just had a crush on him. Her counsellor. Her saviour."

"Fuck, Becca. That's rough."

"Yup. The school have opened or are opening an investigation and all I can do is look through all of his things. Something I felt I'd be able to take my time with as I mourned him. Life is as they say a bitch."

I leaned over, grabbed the bottle and topped up her glass. She looked at it. I could see the debate on her face.

"Becca. Drink the whisky. You said to stop you after a third, this is only your second."

She took a sip. "I don't even know how I find out if Rob was the father. He's been buried. He can hardly supply DNA. And can you tell now, or do you have to wait until the baby is born?"

I pulled out my phone and typed into Google 'Can you do a paternity test before birth?' I clicked into the NHS site's information figuring that would be reliable information.

"You can but it says sometimes you have to go to court for it as it could lead to people requiring terminations. They'd need DNA from Rob, blood test/cheek swab and they need to take fluid from the pregnant woman, an amnio."

"Lengths I'm not prepared to go through for what could be a troubled teenager's imagination, so I guess unless evidence of the possibility turns up in the meantime, I just have to somehow ignore it until such time as she might have a baby. Fucking fabulous." She took another swig.

"Have you checked his emails? His belongings from the school?"

"No. I haven't had time, and school's closed, though the caretaker will be around."

"Well, maybe that's your next steps, and to let the school get on with their investigation, and for now try to concentrate on your new situation which would suck however you lost your husband."

I note Becca's taut jaw.

"Whatever you find out in the future; right now, the husband you loved so very much passed away tragically. You have every right to let yourself go, to mourn his passing, regardless of what information comes forward. Don't block it, Becca. Not facing things just hurts you in other ways."

"It sounds like you're speaking from experience?"

I made a scoffing noise. "Oh you don't want to hear my story, Becca. I'm the villain in my piece."

"Really?" The frown lines were back on Becca's brow. "I find that hard to believe, but then again I barely know you, and then again maybe my whole 'good guy radar' is broken. However, I thought you were talking about your mum. I know from Jules that you've had a secret turn up."

I was such an idiot. Of course she meant about my mum. About my half-brother.

"It's certainly a challenging time. I'm taking Eli bowling Saturday. Trying to get to know him a little better."

"Must be the time for random half-siblings to pop up. That's what Zoey's baby would be. The half-sibling of Laurel. I don't want to know it or her if it's true. Does that make me a heartless bitch? I want my family left alone."

"You're bound to have all sorts of thoughts. Just let them come and then go, Becca. She might not even be pregnant."

"So do you now want to know where your mum is?" Becca's voice rose. "Sorry that was rude of me to blurt that out. You don't have to reply."

"You've just confided in me about your

husband. I have no problems in telling you about my mother."

"Just not about whatever you did in your love life?"

"One secret at a time, hey?"

"Sorry. I might have been widowed but I'm still a nosy bitch with no boundaries."

I laughed. Becca was not what I expected to find tonight at all. Yes, she was grieving; yes, she was troubled; but she certainly didn't pull any punches with people.

"I was nine when mum left. It was devastating. I always said that if she'd died it would have been better. I know that's slightly insensitive given your current situation; but that way you know the outcome, you know they aren't coming back. My mum went and was never heard from again. Now we've found out she had another son and abandoned that child too. What if there are more out there? And you say you wouldn't want anything to do with Zoey's kid if she was pregnant, but that's like my dad telling Eli to get lost. It's not Eli's fault is it?"

Becca finished her second whisky and sat with her head in her hands. "What the fuck am I going to do, Cal?"

I moved closer to Becca on the sofa, putting an arm around her shoulder. Her body shook and I realised she was crying. I held her while her tears flowed until she eventually stopped and pulled away from me, rubbing at her face.

"Sorry. Shit, bet you're so glad you came round." She said, sniffling.

"Let me get you something to wipe your eyes and nose." I'd spotted kitchen roll on the side when we were sorting out our drinks, so I fetched the roll and pulled a sheet off for her.

"Everything is too much for my head. I just need some normal." She pointed to the mail on her coffee table. "I haven't opened those yet. More sympathy cards. If I open them, I have to admit to myself that my husband died and he's never coming back. And also, what if she sent something? What if there's something there I don't want to read?"

"Becca, you don't have to open them today. There's no rulebook on being a widow."

"You mean I don't have to walk around dressed in black for a month?"

"No. Do what you want. Look, why don't you come bowling with us?"

She started to protest.

"Hear me out. Vi's going, along with the rest of us. We're meeting Eli. I think my dad's going to come too. Oh and Angela, Eli's mum. You can bring Laurel, it's family friendly. She'll enjoy all the fuss. You can just either bowl or sit and talk to Vi."

"It's not very seemly to be out so soon after my husband's death, is it?"

"Wear black then." I winked. "Look, you don't have to decide now. It might be too soon, but the offer is there, okay? And I'm sure it will turn into a regular thing because it's a great way for us to get to know Eli better, so anytime you hear we're going from Vi, feel free to tag along."

Becca had drunk her way through a third glass and I could see the alcohol taking effect. Her eyes were drooping with tiredness.

"Right, I'm off, Becca. That's your last drink, so I'll just put the bottle back away in the cupboard for you." She didn't protest as I put it away.

When I returned she was almost asleep on the sofa. But I knew that's not where she'd want to find herself in the morning. "Come on, Becca. Let's get you up to bed."

"Laurel's room." She mumbled. I was confused

for a moment and thought she meant she wanted to know Laurel was okay.

"I'll just check on her for you." I said.

Dashing upstairs, I opened the door of what I knew from the layout of the houses would be the second bedroom, just a fraction. I saw the sofa bed was opened and realised that this was where Becca was sleeping.

Heading back into the living room, I put an arm around Becca and slowly walked upstairs with her. I was sure it was more exhaustion than alcohol affecting her. As carefully and quietly as I could I guided Becca to her sofa bed until she was curled up on it. As I walked past Laurel's small bed, her eyes opened for one brief moment and she said, "Dadda."

My heart shattered. For the dad that wouldn't come home to her beautiful face, for the daughter who wouldn't see her father again, and for the word that would never be uttered to me. Her eyes closed again. I moved stealthily out of the room and left via the front door, posting the keys back through the letterbox. Hoping we had a bottle of whisky in our house because I wasn't done drinking tonight. Not by a long shot.

CHAPTER SEVEN

Becca

"Maaammmmmaaa. Mamamamamamamamam."

I opened one eye slowly. For a moment I wondered where I was, given that the last few days I'd been at my parents' home and now I was in my daughter's bedroom. She was sat up in her bed chattering away happily to herself and my smile broke wide. I was so fucking lucky to have my baby girl.

I got up and opened the blind, letting the day in. It was slightly overcast today. Given the alcohol I'd had last night and the crying I'd done, I was grateful for not being lasered by sunshine.

"Good morning, sweetheart. Want a snuggle with Mummy?"

"Yeah, please." Laurel smiled and climbing out of bed, she got under the covers on my sofa bed and snuggled in at the side of me. I vaguely remembered Cal helping me up here. I should have felt embarrassed, but I didn't appear to possess that gene.

Today was a brand-new day and Laurel was my focus. I'd also tackle the mail, look at Rob's mobile and computer and I would indeed dress in black. Because the street knew I was home now and at least one of them was bound to call around, especially if the gossip was starting to trickle through.

Well, fuck them. I was in mourning but there were indeed no rules and so if they had to sit while I cried on them it served the nosy fuckers right.

Laurel only endured my cuddle for around five minutes before she wanted to get up.

"Milk, Mummy."

"Okay, baby girl."

Damn it. I didn't think we actually had any milk. That was another job for today. Food shopping. I'd do it online. In the meantime, it was going to be another 'rescue me' phone call to Vi, this time asking if she had any spare milk.

"I'm coming round with it. Sit tight." I was going to protest but she carried on talking. "I'm coming and we're chatting about things. I've told Milo I'll be out for a while and that's that."

Not five minutes later, I answered the door to Violet. Her face was flushed and hair escaped from where she'd tried to tie her blonde bob into a ponytail. Milo had obviously kissed the fuck out of her before she left the house. I decided to keep my mouth shut on this occasion.

Her grey eyes swept over me, no doubt assessing the current state of damage.

"I'm sorting Laurel's breakfast so come through. You can put the kettle on, given that I went to sleep last night with the help of three glasses of whisky. I could use a coffee right now." I sucked the side of my cheek. "To be honest, I could use more whisky, but I don't think that would go down well in Parenting 101."

"So I'm guessing Cal got the electrics back on?"

"Yeah, the bulb had blown and tripped the fuse, that was all. If it happens again, I'll know what to do."

"Oh good, you weren't disturbed for too long then."

"Actually, he had a whisky with me. Probably thinks I'm a right dickhead. I needed to talk and he offered an ear."

Vi crossed her arms over her chest. "Um, I thought I told you to ring me if you needed to chat?"

I put some bread in the toaster. "I can't explain it, other than he was someone I didn't really know, and it felt okay to offload on him. I didn't need a response. Like I said, poor guy. He was a dumping ground for my angst and drama. Apologise to him on my behalf, will you?"

"Okay. I'm seeing him tonight. We're taking Eli bowling."

"Yeah, he said. Said I could tag along if I wanted, but I'm not going to." I met Vi's stare. "It's too early for going out anywhere. I need to have my meltdowns in private."

"So was Cal a good listener then? He seems the sort to be. Bit insular. I'd say the most private of the five of them I know."

"He told me he was a villain, about his private life, but then he shut down and wouldn't say anything else..." I left my words trailing for Violet to fill in the answer.

"When I first met Milo, he described Cal as a 'beautiful soul' but he said he jilted his fiancée two years ago."

My mouth gaped open.

"He just found out his ex-fiancée is getting married again. Milo said he hadn't dated for years, but hearing about his ex had him realising it was time to move on."

"And do you know why he did that? Fuck, that poor woman. Did he call off the wedding before the ceremony or..."

"I never told you this, okay?"

I nodded intensely.

"She was left at the altar. Complete drama. I don't know all the details because Milo said it was Cal's story to tell."

I sighed heavily. "I understand. At least I know what his background is now, so if I do bump into him again, I won't put my foot in it."

With Laurel sat eating at the table, Vi and I took a seat at the other end of the table, hot drinks in front of us. I took a sip of coffee and delighted at the taste. It was just what I needed this morning.

. . .

"So how are you doing, really?" Vi kept her voice lowered.

"Shit, my friend. I keep thinking Rob will walk through the door any minute. Then I realise he's gone and I cry. Laurel keeps shouting for him and doesn't understand why he's not there. Then there's all this unknown bollocks about whether he shagged a pupil." I scrubbed a hand through my hair. "Add concerned parents into the mix and I could just pack our bags and disappear." My voice choked with emotion.

Violet moved her chair across the floor so she was nearer my side and put her arm around me, much like Cal had done last night, except she was much smaller and so it was comforting but not as much as Cal's had been. Her hand moved to rub my back a couple of times.

"I'm so sorry, Becca. It's fucking shit, and there's just nothing except time that's going to make it any better. That and of course that lying piece of scum telling the truth."

"But what if she is telling the truth?" I sat up straighter, moving out of Vi's embrace. "I'm going to get the mail that's come and his laptop. Will you help me while I go through everything? Make sure I don't miss anything."

"Sure. Oh I meant to ask, how've you gone on with work? They giving you some time off?"

I shook my head. "Rob had life insurance. I've handed in my notice, effective immediately. It's just one of many things I have to sort out. At least that will help keep me busy, all the paperwork." I looked at my daughter, "and Laurel of course. I'm going to take her out to the park this afternoon. I can't stay cooped up inside forever, and I feel like I need a walk."

"You could pop for some shopping on the way back."

"Not yet. I can't face it if Brenda's there. I don't need all her questions and gossip extraction."

"Fair enough."

I sat and opened the cards and the mail. There was nothing untoward with any of it. It was the same with his laptop and emails. I could turn up nothing that made out a dark and salubrious past.

"It's looking more and more like she made all this up." Vi confirmed what I was feeling myself.

I nodded, sitting back. "It does. I really hope so." For the first time in days I had hope that I could mourn Rob properly. That it was just a matter of time before the school called to apologise. "So how's living with Milo?"

Vi beamed. "It's great so far, although it's very early days."

"And wedding plans?"

"I've told him straight that I'm not getting married until the summer of 2022. I want to take things slow now, after the whirlwind beginning. I'm already twenty-five and divorced once."

My mouth curved in a bemused smirk. "And how did he take to that news?"

"He said the unnerving words, 'We'll see, Princess'."

I burst out laughing. "Watch for holes in the condoms. He'll be trying to get you barefoot and pregnant."

"He's certainly got us practicing enough." She joined in laughing too.

"Hey, there are worse things than marrying the man of your dreams. And you're divorced at twenty-five. I'm widowed at twenty-six."

"Life can be so cruel." She put her hand over mine. "Come on, let's go to the park now. That way, if there's anyone around I can head them off at the pass on your behalf. Let's get you both out of here for a bit."

"Okay." I drank the rest of my coffee down.

"I'll stay with Laurel while you go get a shower."

I hugged my friend, taking her a little by surprise. "Vi, you haven't known me that long and yet here you are, giving me your support. I just want to tell you how much I appreciate it. I really don't know what I'd have done without you this last week or so." Once again emotion choked my words.

She squeezed me in response, her own voice thickening. "I'm here whenever you need me. You understand?"

I nodded.

"Hey, I met you the day after Milo and I'm bloody engaged to him. So looks like I'm the Queen of Fast Relationships. Therefore, we're besties, okay? It's official. I'll get you a friendship bracelet or buy one of those heart pendants, where you keep a half each."

I smiled and headed for the doorway. "I'll be as quick as I can."

"Take your time. I'm not going anywhere." She said. "Me and Laurel are going to have storytime."

The feeling of love and support washed through me as the shower refreshed me and washed away the grogginess of the morning. I thought about those heart pendants. That was how I felt right now. That I only had one half and the other was buried in a local cemetery. I let the shower water join with and wash away my tears before I fixed my brave face and set off for the park.

CHAPTER EIGHT

Callum

"So, Eli. Can you bowl? That is the question." Milo winked at him as we all waited for our bowling shoes.

"I dunno. I haven't been since I was little." Eli replied.

Angela rolled her eyes. "If they're not on an Xbox or their phones, it's odd. Eli is currently having an out of body experience at having to participate in a real life event and not press buttons."

He stuck his tongue out at her.

Dad hovered nearby. "Such a change in the years since I raised kids. I spent a hell of a lot of time stood freezing my arse off while Silas and Finn played football. Then Juliet went to dance classes.

"Don't even go there." Milo growled.

I started laughing. "Aren't we allowed to talk about the time you went to dance class, Miley?"

Violet turned around to look at her fiancé so fast I was surprised her head didn't fall off. "You did what?" Those eyes turned on me. "Tell me right now. I need to know this. Did he do ballet?" She looked at him again. "I can just imagine you in tights."

"I wouldn't be allowed now, Princess. Would be too vulgar with the size of my—" Finally at the last minute he remembered Angela was standing there. "Feet. My feet wouldn't look good in those weird shoe things."

"He did a tap class." Juliet announced. "Always was a weirdo."

"I'd watched Singing in the Rain, leave me alone. Right, are we starting this game or not?" Milo, now having his bowling shoes on stomped off in the direction of our lane.

We ordered food and drinks to come to our lane and half an hour later I was failing dismally at the game but enjoying a pint of beer. Vi came to sit alongside me in the booth.

"Thanks for helping Becca out last night."

I shrugged. "It was no bother. Only a trip."

"I heard you stayed chatting. So again, thank you. She really appreciated it, although she's embarrassed I think for pouring her heart out to the visiting electricity saviour."

"Christ, she's nothing to apologise for. Poor woman just lost her husband, and having a little kid there as well... Bit rough isn't it, what they're accusing her husband of? Not knowing the truth must be torturing her. How can you mourn with all that going on?"

Violet nodded. "I know and it's difficult to know how to help. We went through the mail and Rob's phone and computer today and there was nothing. It's all on the school now to find some concrete evidence. She really doesn't need this."

"I wish she'd have come out tonight. I get she's newly widowed, but this would have been a distraction. She could have just talked with you."

"Yeah, but she only just buried her husband. It's hard to know what must be going on in her head. I understand her need to stay home with

Laurel and just lie low. We went to the park this morning though, so she's been out."

"Oh that's good."

"It was, because we didn't bump into anyone we knew, so she was able to enjoy some fresh air and we chatted while Laurel made a friend on the swings."

"I honestly don't know how you're supposed to get over someone so close dying. Especially at that young age."

"I know. He was thirty. In some ways it's good that Laurel's so young isn't it?"

"Yeah, I guess."

"God, sorry, Cal, we've come out for some fun and to get to know Eli and here we are all gloomy, talking about Becca. Tell me about you. How's things going?"

"My life's as exciting as ever. I've been working, as you know because you give me the jobs to go to, and then, well, the most exciting part of my week was turning the fuse switch back on."

"Oh, Cal. You need a date. Did nothing happen with Lisa at the pub?"

"Nope. I tried to talk to her and she turned the conversation to Ezra and asked if I'd heard how he was doing. I took it as she wasn't interested."

Violet wringed her hands and turned to look at the bowlers. "It takes forever to get a turn when there are so many of us."

"Yeah, this game could last some time. Especially when your other half has to do his macho posturing and bending before he takes a turn."

"Which is doing nothing at all because Silas just walked up, bowled, and got a strike. My boyfriend is not looking as cocky now."

I turned to look as Silas saluted Milo and walked off back over to where Eli stood.

"So, are you going to try and explore other dating avenues? There are dating sites and apps."

"I don't feel that desperate yet." I laughed. "I'd rather do things the normal way. There's really no rush. I'm not sure what I have to offer anyone anyway."

"*Callum Waite.* You have lots to offer someone."

"Princess! Come and have your turn and quit harping on like a fishwife."

"Ooooohh." Violet's feathers were ruffled. "If there is a God, he'll let me get a strike." She shouted. "Don't care, Princess. Worth losing to just see you bending over in those tight jeans." Milo shouted back. The family at the next booth looked over. The dad laughed, the mother gave him a prod to the arm, clearly telling him not to be so overt in nosying at us. It was hard not to look at us when we had Milo Waite strutting and Juliet with her bright blue hair and piercings. People assumed stuff about Jules because of her appearance. Stereotypical stuff that wasn't her at all. So far she'd spent the evening chatting to Angela and Eli.

I got up and took my turn after Vi. My first attempt went down the gutter and my second knocked three pins down. A bowling talent I was not. But I'd thought it would be a good place for us all to mix and it seemed to be going well.

Vi came back to sit at the side of me, but this time Milo followed. "What's happening here? You decided you prefer this skinny whippet version of me? Do I need to diet?"

"No, we're just chatting, about dating." Milo's eyes swept over me. He knew my truths and despite being a gobshite had kept them to himself. I'd wondered if he'd told Violet. I'd have understood if he had, but she didn't appear to know. Her conversation and behaviour weren't hinting at that. But then if I had someone, I'd have shared everything with them, so maybe she was just keeping it to herself and knew everything after all.

"So, I'm going to be blunt here, Cal. Do you still have feelings for your ex? Are you still in love with her and that's why you're not dating anyone else? Because if so, you need to go talk to her. What if she doesn't love this new fiancé as much as she loved you?" She took a deep breath. "There, I said it. Sorry, but you need to be able to move on somehow. Why didn't you go through with the wedding?"

Okkkkaaayyy, so she did know. Just not all of it. I looked around, making sure no one had overheard her.

"Fucking hell, Princess. You've made me look like a delicate flower." Milo's eyes were wide looking at his girlfriend.

"Sod it, I'm basically family. I want to help." She placed a hand on the top of my arm. "You were there for me, same saviour like Becca last night. Made sure my house was safe for me. I'm there for you. I want you to know that."

I decided to tell her the truth. "I was going to end things because I couldn't have children."

Vi gasped. "Oh fuck, Callum, I'm so sorry."

"I do feel like there's unfinished business with her, but I'm sure we wouldn't have worked anyway. Just sometimes I find it unfair that everyone points fingers at me because I didn't turn up at the altar."

"Because you can't have children and kind of did it for the right reasons?"

I nodded. "And because her father had me kidnapped and held in an outbuilding until I wrote a note finishing our relationship." I confessed.

There was a stunned silence from Violet. "What? Fuck, Cal. I know Milo said there was more to it, but I didn't expect it to be that. Did you go to see her afterwards? To explain what he'd done? Surely, she should know the truth?"

"It didn't matter. I'd been going to tell her I'd overheard she didn't want to adopt. She was having second thoughts but felt it was too late to cancel. Her father saved me the bother."

There it all was, my truths, bowled out. Strike for Callum Waite. I felt like the pins. Hit hard and knocked over.

Violet pulled me into her arms. "I'm sorry for pushing, Cal. Please forgive me. I thought you still loved her. Thought I could maybe get you to go see her before it was too late..."

"Don't sweat it, Vi. You're right. I do need to see her. I've wondered about telling her the truth for a while. But I haven't because ultimately what good does it do?"

Violet pulled back. "It gives you closure. Like when I went to see my mum. It can help you move on. And what about your ex? Maybe it's given her issues that you could draw a line under?"

"Yeah, perhaps it's time. Then she can get married and live happily ever after, eh?"

It was there in the loved-up Vi's face. The possibility of some kind of fairy tale where the exes reunited and lived happily ever after. A possibility she'd not thought could happen for herself until recently, now became achievable for anyone else.

I didn't know how I'd manage to get near enough to speak to Tali. I'd been blocked on her social media a long time ago, but somehow, I'd make the effort and get that final closure Vi spoke of because maybe it was that which stopped me moving on. Maybe I made my not being able to have a kid my excuse to not face up to the disaster which had been my wedding day.

"Okay, excuse me. I'm going to go choose a different ball because I can't get three pins again. I'm coming last, look." All three of us looked at the board. "If I just get a few more I can beat Angela at least."

"Yeah, it's pitiful. Angela's not the slightest bit interested. She just basically keeps lobbing hers down and going back to chat with everyone before she's even looked at what score she's got." Milo added helpfully.

"Her and Dad seem deep in conversation."

"Got a lot to talk about, haven't they? Eli's asked if he can come and stay for a few days with it being the school holidays."

I left Milo and Vi chatting and went over to one of the main racks holding all the bowls. After trying a few I could see I needed a size that wasn't on this rack so I began to wander up towards the next one. My hand reached out for the correct ball and then I heard a, "Callum?"

As I stood up and looked into the eyes of Tali, my ex, I wondered if I was dreaming. How could I be seeing her here now after we'd just been talking about her? Reality showed she really was there though as the shock caused me to lose my grip and the bowling ball hit my foot.

CHAPTER NINE

Becca

I'd felt so much better after the walk to the park. Vi had been right to make me go out and Laurel had loved it, making friends and running around, her breakfast and sleep having given her a ton of energy. Maybe soon it would be time to consider a part-time nursery place for her. She was three in mid-September. I needed to look and see what was available. I knew my parents loved looking after her while I did my part-time job, but there was something to be gained from being able to hang around with kids her own age, and we only had one toddler group around here on a Monday that my mum and dad had taken her to. Now that would be me. I'd never really been one for groups and polite chit chat. The whole thing made me feel icky, so maybe a nursery placement would work better or a childminder. Then I only had the drop off and collection to suffer.

But then there'd be birthday parties.

And playdates.

Looked like my life was most definitely having a complete upheaval. Did Becca Staveley have to actually become sociable?

My phone began ringing with an unknown number. Usually, I wouldn't answer, but right now I didn't know if it could be important. I'd had many strange numbers ringing lately, due to my dealing with funeral directors etc, so I pressed accept and brought it to my ear.

"H- hello."

"Mrs Staveley?"

"Yes?"

"It's Roger Dexter, Rebecca. Are you okay to talk?"

Roger Dexter, the Head of Rob's school. It was a moment that seemed like a lifetime. My past of either truth or lies lay before me.

"Yes, I can talk."

"How are you doing?"

False platitudes. I had run out of patience for them. I wanted to know the truth.

"What's the verdict on my husband? I guess that's why you're calling."

"Erm, yes, I've been in to school due to the circumstances. We had Zoey in and her mother, and well, Zoey is not pregnant. Not in the slightest."

I breathed out, a slow exhale that felt like every muscle and fibre of my body began to loosen.

"So did she admit to lying?"

"No, unfortunately she was adamant that she was telling the truth about a sexual relationship with your husband, but there is no evidence. She couldn't provide any. We're getting her some additional help as she is in quite a state."

"Her and me both."

"Anyway, I thought I'd let you know that as far as the school are concerned that's the end of the matter and Zoey's mum asked me to pass on her condolences and her deepest apologies and asked that you bore in mind that Zoey has issues."

"Is that everything?"

"Just to ask you about Rob's locker. Do you want the contents? We can box them up and send them to you?"

"I'd appreciate that. Thank you."

"You understand that we had to follow this through and look into it, Rebecca? I'm sorry for the intrusion on your grieving. We all will dearly miss Rob."

"I have to go now; my daughter is shouting for me." I hung up. They'd dearly miss my husband who they thought was abusing a pupil. Yes, I understood what they'd had to do, but what I didn't have to do was listen to them anymore.

Now I could mourn my husband properly and hope if he was watching he forgave me for ever doubting him. I couldn't deny to myself that a small percentage had wondered if Zoey was telling the truth. She was a fucking good liar, I'd give her that. I only hoped that they found someone else who could get her on a better path in life.

Now, I would take each day at a time, the way we could only ever really live, in the moment, and hope time indeed was a healer.

Thinking that I wanted to feel closer to Rob, but that I needed to do something to accept he was no longer here, I decided to go through his clothes, and began to fill a charity bag. Laurel was napping and so I had the time. Rob had always had his favourite clothes and only ever wore about a third of his wardrobe anyway, so I could get rid of the things he'd never really worn now and then take my time accepting letting go of the ones that would bring me different memories as I held them in my hands.

He'd been buried in his wedding suit. It had still fitted him perfectly, which made me smile because I'd be lucky if I could get one leg inside my wedding dress. Childbirth changed a woman's body, and I personally wouldn't change a thing. I'd much rather have the womanly curves I had now, that extra pound or two on my midriff and my bottom, than be the skinny minny of my wedding day where I'd dieted to look as amazing as I felt possible; some version of myself that youth and vanity had made me strive for.

I packed up his summer clothes first. The ones Rob only ever took on holiday. Loud coloured t-shirts that were emblazoned with words like Ibiza 1982. Shorts that would induce a migraine. There was no smell of Rob around these clothes, just a fustiness and I threw them into the black sack with ease. I stared at the wardrobe wondering what to do next. The irony of the black suit hanging in the wardrobe was not lost on me. Rob's funeral suit. Last worn to his father's. Never to be worn again, while in other people's wardrobes similar black suits hung, last worn to his.

I pulled it out of the wardrobe, folding up the jacket and placing it in the bag. Pulling the trousers from the hanger I felt a padding in the pocket. A wallet. I took it out and opened it to see if there was anything inside, any hidden money long forgotten about. I could see the edge of photographs and sitting myself against the bed, I extracted them and prepared for an onslaught of memories.

But that wasn't what I got.

As my body began to retch, as my world began to spin and whirl, my mind caught up to the images. The images of four different teenage girls posing nude for the camera, for the Polaroid pictures, one who was clearly Zoey. I lost my grip on reality and blackness consumed me.

CHAPTER TEN

Callum

I didn't get chance to talk further to Tali due to a mass exodus of the Waite family.

"Callum, there's an emergency. We're off." Milo growled, alongside Vi, and Jules.

I searched their faces to try to read what was happening. "What the fuck happened?"

"Becca's called Vi. She found something about her husband. She's in pieces. We're going to see what we can do to help."

"I'm coming."

It was then I noticed that Tali had gone. No doubt as soon as my siblings had approached. Perhaps we weren't ever meant to have a conversation to clear the air after all. I had no further time to think on it as I collected my shoes and got the hell out of there with my family.

"Dad, Silas, and Finn are staying to finish the game with Eli and Angela. We just told them Becca needed us. They think it's a grief thing."

I wasn't sure why I'd been included in the rescue group. Vi and Jules were her friends and Milo went where Vi went. Obviously, the fact we'd chatted last night now meant I was Team Becca.

"So what's happened?" I asked while Milo drove us back to their house.

"I could hardly make out a word she said, but she mentioned finding some photographs and that she didn't know what to do." Vi twisted a strand of hair, her foot bouncing as if it might help get us there faster.

The ten-minute journey seemed to take much longer, but eventually Milo pulled up outside their house. Jules and Vi leapt out. "You girls see what's happening and call us if you need us." Milo said kissing his fiancée's cheek. Vi nodded at him, her forehead wrinkled, and then her and Jules went running up Becca's path.

"So what do we do?" I asked my brother as he locked the car and leant against it.

"Wait a few minutes, see if they need us and if not, go see a very fussy dog."

"Okay."

Within a couple of minutes, Milo's phone started ringing. He listened, said "Okay," and nodding his head he started walking in the direction of Becca's house.

"It's bad and none of them know what to do. Let's go see what's going on."

"Fuck." Was the only response I could think to give, and I followed my brother up to Becca's front door where Jules let us inside, rubbing at her brow.

"We don't know what we're supposed to do. Ring the police or what? Come, listen, and help."

The word police had me on full alert. What the fuck had she found? I don't know what came over me, but I pushed past Milo and strode into the living room.

What I saw devastated me. Becca was hysterical. On her knees on the living room floor with Violet's arm around her as she sobbed and spoke words I couldn't fully make out. Little Laurel looked bewildered, crying herself and clutching at Becca who seemed to be desperately trying to soothe her baby girl, smoothing her hair.

Laurel looked at Milo and then me and shouted, "Daddy."

We all froze.

Becca spoke through hitched breaths. "She's at th-that age. Ev-very man d-daddy."

Moving forward, I scooped Laurel up into my arms. "Hello, baby girl. Shall we go look for butterflies in the garden?"

She nodded her head, "Budderfly."

"I'll come with you." Jules added and she walked with me through to the kitchen, unlocking the back door so I could step outside with Laurel.

The little tiny body in my arms was warm and wriggly as she turned looking for butterflies. A gasp of pain came at the fact I might never experience this for myself. A little ball of wonder, innocence personified, trusting the person who held her, while looking for the magic in the world. Jules searched the garden, and I could see she was almost praying for a butterfly to appear, but there was nothing. I thought back to my childhood and remembered my own mother, when she was home and gave a shit. Sitting in the garden with Jules and making daisy chains. I looked at the unmown grass. Bingo.

"Jules." I called her. "Daisy chains."

A look of relief hit my sister's features. "Yes!" I put Laurel down and sat next to her and Jules rushed over plucking a daisy from the grass. "Laurel. Let me make you a daisy chain." Laurel's chubby little hand reached for the daisy in Jules' hand and Jules let her have it.

"Flower."

"Yes, Laurel, pretty flower."

While Jules made a daisy chain, I kept passing the odd daisy to Laurel who was pulling petals off and throwing them around. She'd get up and go pull one up herself, along with a clump of grass and come show us, earning praise for her endeavours. And while she was busy, Jules told me about what Becca had found. I wanted to be sick.

"How the fuck is she supposed to process that? Her husband, who she was madly in love with, took advantage of young girls. She doesn't know if they were all sixteen. Even so, even if they were over the age of consent, he still abused his position as a counsellor at school."

"So she needs to phone the police or contact the school."

Jules shrugged. "We don't know what to do, that's the problem. Need to do some Googling, but first we have to get Becca to calm down. She could do with some meds, but the doctors are emergencies only at weekends and she won't take anything because of Laurel anyway."

I took my phone out of my pocket. "Let's see if I can find anything while we're out here."

"Your search history is gonna be a bit dubious."

"Yeah, well, anything that can help."

All I come up with is information from the NSPCC about it being against the law for people working in school to have sexual relations with children, even if they were over the age of consent, and that not every role was covered and so they were on a mission to close loopholes.

"It seems like she needs to contact the Head so they can activate their child safeguarding procedures. There's no point calling the police because Rob's dead, so he's no longer a danger to these kids." I sigh. "Not in body anyway. Only hell knows what damage he's done to them psychologically."

Jules bit her lip. "And they were vulnerable anyway. That's why they were seeing him. It's disgusting. How the hell is Becca supposed to get her head around any of this? She's lost her husband and found out all this."

"She's going to need a counsellor herself."

"What a mess." Jules sighed and we returned to making daisy chains and entertaining Laurel.

A while later, Violet came outside to get Laurel.

"How is she?" Jules asked.

"Not good. She won't call her parents who we think she needs right now. She's agreed to come and stay at ours tonight. Milo's said he'll go in the spare room so me, Becca, and Laurel can sleep in our bed. I guess she needs to wait until she's called the headteacher. There's no quick fix here." She turned to Laurel. "Let's go back to Mummy. Bring your daisies."

"That's our cue to leave." Jules looked at me and I nodded back. As we returned to the living room, Becca's gaze met mine before she quickly looked away. Her eyes were swollen to the point of almost being shut. Jules touched her arm. "If you need either of us for anything, you just call, okay?"

Becca nodded. "Thank you for being here." She looked around, her eyes filling with tears again. "All of you."

Without thinking, I stepped forward and took her into my arms. Her body collapsed against me as she broke down once more. "We're all here for you." I murmured into her hair. "Every one of us.

Do not feel embarrassed because of what that shit of a husband did."

Violet approached, a look on her face that said, 'you can step away' now. I passed Becca to her arms and walked out, Milo following me.

"What was that all about?"

"What?" I shrugged.

"Listen, bro. I'm King of rescuing princesses, remember? That seemed a lot like swooping in to save the damsel in distress."

"Just feel really sorry for her. Got to be rough, with having the little kid and all."

He raised a brow, but he didn't challenge me any further. I left him at his front door and I walked around the side of his house, cut through the garden and went back to mine.

And entered another drama. The rest of the family were back and my new little brother seemed to be making his presence known.

"I want to stay here for a week. You can't stop me." He screeched at Angela, who stood with her hands on her hips. My dad stood there looking like he wanted to be anywhere but here.

"Eli. You can't just invite yourself into someone else's home, and also, we need to sort this properly. I'd rather we spoke about this at home and then you let me speak to Josh."

"He said I could stay. Didn't you, Mr. Waite? I have a room and everything."

"It has to be with your mother's agreement."

"She's not my mum." He yelled and I heard Finn's sharp intake of breath. "Right, buddy, let's me and you go for a walk around the block." He grabbed Eli's arm. "C'mon, Callum. You can come too."

So much for some time to get my head together. In one evening, I'd seen my ex, been witness to Becca's horrendous situation, and now things were kicking off under my own roof. Shame Eli wasn't over eighteen because I could really use a drink.

I sighed. "Okay, let's go. Time to find out having brothers isn't all sweetness and light, young man." I folded my arms across my chest looking at a pouting Eli. I gave Angela a sympathetic smile. "We'll be back soon. I'll leave my dad to get you a drink and reassure you about dealing with stroppy teenagers. He had enough of us."

Angela smiled back, although her eyes were definitely looking a bit glassy. I followed my brothers out of the house. What a day.

. . .

"Let's head to the park." I told Finn and Eli. Of course, Eli hadn't been there before, so he just walked alongside us.

"I know you've brought me out here to give me a lecture about being rude to Angela, but she needs to realise you're my family."

"No, mate. What you need to realise is our real mother is a complete turd." I snapped, seeing Finn's head snap towards me in shock, his eyes wide. I stopped and turned to Eli. "Angela is amazing. I've only met her twice and I can see that. This woman has stayed by your side even though she has no biological attachment to you whatsoever. You should be proud to call her your mum, not insult her like you just did back at the house."

Eli's head dropped as his shoulders slumped.

"Steady on, Cal. Lad's just trying to adjust to everything."

I took a deep inhale. "I'm sorry I yelled. It's been quite the day." I put my arm around Eli. "Seriously, little bro, you can't treat your mum like that. She's been a constant for you all these years, and yes, she fully understands you want to spend time with us, but she's making sure it's organised properly. That's what mum's are supposed to do. Don't forget that our dad is not yours. It's all a bit awkward."

"Does your dad not want me around?" Panic flooded Eli's gaze.

"Dad's fine with you staying. It must be difficult for him though. You're the product of the affair that took our mum away, but dad understands that's not your fault and he wants to get to know you as much as we do. But Dad will insist this is done the right way, with your mum's full permission and not with you throwing yourself about saying you can do what you like."

"I just really want to hang with you guys and get to know you better and I can do that if I come stay."

I ruffled his hair. We were just reaching the park and I pointed towards the zip wire. "Come on, let's go burn some of your energy off. Then we can go back and you can apologise, and then, we can *negotiate*," I stressed the word out to Eli, "you staying at ours before you go back to school for the Autumn term."

"Okay." Eli nodded. He walked on ahead in his excitement to go first on the zip wire.

"You're good with him." Finn said. That's why I asked you to come out with us. I didn't have a fucking clue what I was going to say other than quit being a drama queen."

"When he's gone home, do you fancy coming back out for a pint?"

"Was going to ask you the same thing. It's been quite a day hasn't it? You can tell me what's been happening at Becca's."

"I can also tell you that just before the drama happened with Becca, I ran into Tali at the bowling alley."

"What? Fuck, what did she say?"

"She didn't get to say anything. Milo and the rest came and collected me to go to Becca's. When I turned back, she'd gone."

"How did she look?"

"Surprised to see me, but good. She looked good." I couldn't deny it. She'd always been beautiful and that hadn't changed.

"Let's get Eli back and home with Angela, and then you'd best catch me up with everything." He said. "It's never boring with us lot, is it?"

I huffed. "Nope."

CHAPTER ELEVEN

Becca

On the Saturday night and Sunday, I'd been in a state of shock, but by Monday morning, I'd called Roger Dexter and arranged to meet him at school. I actually felt guilty I was disturbing his summer break, but then again my whole life was being ripped apart.

Violet had arranged to go into work late so that she could look after Laurel for me. I hated how much I was inconveniencing other people, but what could I do? It wasn't appropriate to take her with me.

"I don't know how to say this, so I'm just going to put these here." I pushed an envelope containing the photos across the desk. "I'm going to tell you the contents so that you don't have to look at them." I breathed deep, trying to keep it together, while the headteacher waited for more of my words. "There are four photographs in there, Mr Dexter. Four Polaroids of four different pupils. One is Zoey. She was telling some truth it would seem. They're all naked."

Mr Dexter gasped. His hand covering his mouth.

I sat up straight, typical British stiff upper lip on display, even though I wanted to crumple to my feet and just give up on everything. "I've searched the house from top to bottom. I can't find anything else. I know you'll have procedures to follow now. I'll help in whatever way I can."

He nodded.

I stood up. "It doesn't help anyone, and you don't have to believe me, but I didn't know. I promise you. I would never have stayed with a man capable of doing such things if I'd have known. I would have reported him. Now I somehow have to live with the truth of who he was, or the fact I didn't know who he really was, while I mourn a man who didn't really exist."

Mr Dexter stood up also. "I'm sorry, Mrs Staveley. This must be very difficult, but I now need to contact the authorities."

Leave. That's what he was saying.

I nodded and then I walked away. I'd just dropped a lit fuse and now it would ignite and blow through Willowfield.

When I went back to Vi's I felt battered and bruised. I just wanted to retreat from the world.

"What did they say?" She asked me as I picked up Laurel and hugged her close. She immediately wiggled to be put down. She wanted to play with Rocky, not cuddle me.

"He's starting an investigation. Now I just have to wait."

"Well, you know you can stay here as long as you like. Do you fancy a drink?"

I shook my head.

"Thank you for everything you've done, but I just want to go back home. I'm going to pack up our things and make my way back. I just need some time to think."

"I understand."

So I returned to my house, a place that no longer felt like home. It was only a couple of hours later that there was a knock at the door and I opened it to find the police on my doorstep. They showed me their ID and I invited them inside. There was a man and a woman. I didn't take much notice of their names. I just wanted them gone.

"I'm sorry for your loss. We understand this must be very difficult for you right now." The policewoman said.

"It's agony." I blurted out truthfully. "Complete and utter agony, because I'm the one left behind to deal with it."

They both nodded in a sympathetic way before the guy spoke. "We need to go through your husband's belongings, especially things like his phone, laptop, etc."

"So what happens?" I asked. "Seeing as he's dead."

"Our main concern is if there were other victims as well as the four girls in the photographs at this stage."

I stood up. "Let me show you all his belongings so you can take what you need."

Once they were ready to leave they asked if I would be going anywhere in case they had further questions.

"I might end up back at my parents' house, but

I'll make sure I always have my mobile phone so that you can reach me."

When I closed the door behind them, I allowed my grief to hit me. Hot tears flooded my cheeks as my knees hit the carpet below my feet. I cried until I felt spent and exhausted, but there was no rest for me. Anger hit me from nowhere.

Knowing the police had taken everything they needed, I dragged out a storage box from under my bed, emptying the photos out of it. In here I would put a few items for Laurel when she was older, but everything else I needed gone.

While Laurel had a nap I went through his things. Every book he'd owned, every CD he'd played, every DVD he'd watched, I threw them in a black sack. Watches I'd bought him. Photos of us together or him alone I put in a pile on the floor. I kept some family ones and placed them in the storage box, alongside some of just Laurel and Rob. Anything he'd had passed down to him like a signet ring from his grandfather I placed in the box for Laurel. Yes, his belongings could have gone to charity, but I needed the satisfaction of dumping them. I opened the black bin and threw them inside. Then I grabbed a box of matches and the photographs. I gathered some twigs and I put the photos across them. Then I threw turps on them that we'd had in from painting. Standing back because I knew it would ignite with force, I threw a match on and as the flames whooshed I felt a sick sense of satisfaction in seeing Rob burn.

"You fucking idiot." I yelled. "How could you? How could you do this to me and especially to Laurel, you utter, utter bastard." I yelled. Grabbing a sweeping brush leant against the wall, I lifted and smashed it into the burning pile. Fury burned through me hotter than the fire and the next thing I knew I'd smashed the brush straight through a garden ornament Rob had bought.

I jumped out of my skin as arms came around me, pulling the brush from my hand and discarding it to the ground. I hit out in self defence against the person trying to stop me.

"Fuck, Becca, that hurt. Stop. Please just stop."

Recognising the voice, the fight went out of me and I fell onto the grass, breathing heavy from all the exertion.

Callum stood in front of me, his eyes checking me over as if I might be injured. Oh I was injured alright, but it wasn't my body. My injuries weren't anything an eye could see.

"I heard you screaming. I flew down the side of

Vi's and up the side of yours. What's going on? Has something else happened?" He looked at the small fire and the shattered ornament.

"Fuck, I'd better get this cleaned up. Laurel could injure herself." I got back to my feet. "Damn it, I've probably woken her up anyway. I need to check on her."

"Stop." Callum's hands were on my arms, blocking my path. "We need to sort you out first. We can clear the path after. I'll check on Laurel."

"Callum, go back to work. I'm fine. I just needed to do some clearing up of Rob's things." I shrugged him off me and went into the kitchen. He pushed past me and went to check on Laurel.

"She's still asleep." He informed me not a minute later.

"Good. It's the best thing for her right now. Not to witness her mother having a meltdown." The irony of using a sweeping brush to smash up an ornament and make some mess suddenly amused me and stopping, I burst into a peal of laughter, and then another as I took in Callum's wary expression. He thought I'd cracked up clearly, and maybe I had.

"What's happened today?" He said, no amusement on his own face.

"Nothing unusual, you know, just went to school and told the headteacher my dead husband was an abuser and then entertained a couple of police officers. Finished it all off with a clear out, hence the fire."

Suddenly, I saw myself through Callum's eyes. Unhinged. I slumped onto a seat at the kitchen table. "I can't escape this shit show, Callum. What the fuck am I supposed to do?"

He took the seat next to me and sucked on his top lip for a moment.

"I don't know, Becca. I wish I had an answer for you, but I don't."

I sighed.

"But I can make a really good cup of tea, and I'm fab at cleaning up, so why don't you sit tight and I'll sort out the mess out there while you have a hot drink and try to calm down before Laurel wakes up?"

Nodding, I stayed in my seat and pointed to the cupboard under the sink where the dustpan and brush were kept. My energy was depleted, and I could hardly keep my eyes open.

"I can't stay in this house. I need to put it up for sale and move somewhere else."

"Where would you go?" He asked me.

"Probably nearer to my parents. It makes sense."

"Becca, you've just lost your husband, found out all this other stuff. Don't rush to put your house on the market." He frowned. "Is there anywhere you can stay awhile? Is back with your parents an option? You need time to grieve. It's not the right time to make huge decisions about your future."

"Maybe. I don't know. I'm so fucking tired, Callum. So fucking tired." I slumped my head back. "And now my whirlwind of a two-year-old will want to play."

"I'll help you keep Laurel occupied. I got my job completed early so I'm free the rest of the day."

Once again, I had neighbours helping. It wasn't right. "I'm going to call my parents tonight and see if I can stay with them for a while. I think it's for the best."

"Are you sure, because I don't mind helping you at all, none of us do. You have friends here, Becca."

"I know. I just think it's for the best. Any minute the news about Rob will get out and the gossip will start. Then how will it be?"

"I'd not thought of that."

For a fleeting moment I wished Rob had never

turned up for our blind date. What would have happened with the man currently helping me now?

I closed my eyes. I wouldn't have had my daughter. My beautiful daughter who was my world. And this man had his demons too. I didn't really know Callum Waite.

It struck me then, that at some point in the far away distance of life, people would expect me to date again. How the hell would I ever trust another soul? No. My heart was locked and sealed away for any romantic love. All my love would go on my daughter and in giving her the world.

"You're a good friend, Callum Waite." I told him and watched as he smiled at me.

"I'm glad you think so. And not that I'm just a nosy git sticking my oar in your business. We all just want to support you, Becca. We've been through our own share of drama have us Waites."

"Would it be okay as a mate to ask if you want to have some Chinese with us tonight?" I was being selfish in asking I knew, but he helped me escape all the thoughts in my head.

"Sounds good to me."

I smiled. That would pass the time until bedtime and then tomorrow, I would call my parents. I knew they'd not hesitate to let me come back. They'd not wanted me to leave in the first place. But if for some reason, they'd changed their mind, I'd book us into a hotel nearby, because I needed to get us away from Willowfield until Rob became yesterday's fish and chip paper, rather than Guy Fawkes.

CHAPTER TWELVE

Callum

Poor Becca and poor Laurel. What awful circumstances to be trying to cope with right now. The least I could do was say yes to a Chinese and try to distract them for a short while. Becca went to wake Laurel and brought a sleepy little girl downstairs. As soon as she saw me, her eyes brightened and Laurel immediately shouted "Daisy," having remembered the last time I'd entertained her.

"Come on then, squirt. Although I'm not sure I can actually make them." I recalled that last time Laurel hadn't so much wanted a bracelet as to shred them to bits. That I could manage.

“You give your parents a ring while I entertain the little one.” I suggested to Becca.

"Okay." Picking up her phone, she went back into the kitchen, watching us through the window while she spoke.

Laurel was a picture of innocence as she moved around the garden from one thing to another, laughing and giggling as she went. I felt terribly sorry she had to live without her daddy. I knew what losing a parent was like, even if mine hadn’t died. Even though Laurel was young, as she got older she’d want to know all about him. No doubt Becca would have more problems to come with time.

Becca walked out into the garden and sat down on the grass at the side of me. “All sorted. We move back in with my parents tomorrow for as long as we like.”

“That’s good. They’ll no doubt love having Laurel around.”

“Yeah. They adore her.”

“It’s not hard to see why. She’s a gorgeous little thing.”

“Well, I think so, but I’m biased.”

We played with Laurel until hunger pangs hit and then we ordered the Chinese.

"Tell me what happened with your ex." Becca blurted. I froze, a piece of lemon chicken in front of my mouth. "Vi said you bumped into her again the other day. Please tell me something. I promise not to tell anyone, even Vi. I just need something to distract me from my own shit storm."

I put the chicken in my mouth and chewed. Did I really want to talk about this? I looked at Becca. The truth was I had a feeling that once I began to open up to her, it would all pour out. Becca wasn't the sort of person who'd let you short change her. I knew she'd question and push at me for answers if I began to tell my tale. But how could I say no to the person currently going through what she was going through?

"I left my ex at the altar on our wedding day." I said, waiting for a gasp that didn't come. So she did know then, no doubt courtesy of Vi. I wondered how much of it Vi had told her. Looked like soon I'd be wise to tell the rest of my family what I was about to tell Becca. They'd been patient with me, but finding out I told a relative stranger before them wouldn't go down well if I didn't and somehow the truth came out. "I had my reasons."

"Which were?" She pressed.

"If I tell you, you need to hear the whole of it. Beginning to end."

"That's fine," she said, so I began.

"I met Tali in a nightclub when I was nineteen. She was a year younger. To cut a long story short, we fell in love and I proposed. Her father never liked me and so I never asked his permission to marry her, because I knew he wouldn't have given it."

"Why did he not like you?"

"Because to him I had no prospects. Tali's father was a successful businessman who travelled the world and worked in finance. They lived in a large detached house in Danesford where the driveway was so long it took ten minutes to reach the front door. I was a trainee electrician in Willowfield and although it was a family firm, I discovered that it wasn't anything he wanted his grandchildren to inherit. It wasn't seemly."

"He told you this?" Becca looked astounded.

"Eventually, yes." I confirmed, "but there's a lot more to this story yet."

She nodded for me to continue.

"So the wedding was booked for in eighteen

months time, everything was going ahead, invites were out, the honeymoon was arranged. Everything, and we're in love and looking forward to the rest of our lives. We were living in a rented property and Tali had been going on about having children. Her friends were having babies left, right, and centre and she was talking about us having a kid before the wedding. It was too soon for me, we were both so young. In the back of my mind, I'd still been hoping to win her dad around by working hard and making a name for myself, getting a good reputation and trying to save for a house in a better area. I didn't think getting her pregnant before the wedding would go down well.

"Quite."

"Time passed, the wedding got nearer, and I decided I wanted to get Tali some sexy lingerie for on our honeymoon, so I went in her undies drawer to check out her sizes. I found a pregnancy testing kit, and I just knew, in my gut, that she'd not been taking her pill. That despite what I'd said she was trying to get pregnant.

"I called her out on it, and she sobbed and apologised but said she needed to have a child so badly, it had overridden everything else. Her biological clock was ticking to the point of explosion she said.

After we'd talked, I thought, why am I holding off just to please her father? I should be doing what my wife-to-be wants and if we had to postpone the wedding or she had to walk down the aisle with a bump then so be it because it was Cal and Tali, and we were perfect.

"Nothing happened and I put it down to the stress of the wedding, but I heard Tali talking to a friend and saying how every month that passed made her feel like she was mourning. I told her we'd get tested, make sure everything was okay. Except it wasn't. I found out I couldn't have children."

My eyes went to the floor as I told Becca my truths.

"Oh, Callum, I am so very sorry."

I swallowed. "She said she was okay with it. That there were other options. I told her she could cancel the wedding. Could leave me. She said no; that we'd get through it."

"I'm guessing it didn't go that way?"

I carried on staring into space as I remembered my past. "It was a lie. She had pregnancy magazines that she kept. I watched as her friends with babies visited and she pretended to be okay and then I'd hear her sob at night. Two days before the wedding I heard her on the phone to her best friend saying that she wasn't sure she could adopt after all. That she'd always imagined her own children, and that the more she explored adoption, the more she found horror stories where they'd gone wrong. I heard her say that it was too late now to cancel the wedding and that she just felt trapped. Hearing her say that cut me deep, but yet I understood.

"After mulling things over that night, I'd decided that the following day I would talk to her and even though it would break my heart, if she wanted, we would call the wedding off. I spent that next day trying to work up the courage to start a conversation that I knew might end us, but I just couldn't do it. Then I found myself bundled into the back of a car and taken to an outbuilding and it was all taken out of my hands."

"*What?*"

"I'd been on my way to meet Milo. I was staying with him in a hotel the night before the wedding with him being my best man. The guy had fucking taken me off our driveway. As I was thrown into the outbuilding, I found her father sitting there looking smug. Her best friend had contacted him and told him how Tali was feeling.

The fact I couldn't help provide him with a biological heir was the final straw for him. He told me he didn't want some adopted riff raff.

"What an arsehole."

"I was made to write a note. He threatened to hurt Jules if I didn't write it. So I did. Figured fate had decided Tali was better off without me anyway. He took the note and his goons let me go. I was warned if I went anywhere near the church, Jules would be left in a bad way."

"Jesus, Callum."

"And so when Milo came to stay, I didn't say a word, and when he got up the next morning, I wasn't there.

"I'd booked myself on a train to Edinburgh. Far, far away from the wedding that wasn't to happen." My tale was pouring out of me now, the wound wide open and I was bleeding out. "I knew how her father was going to break the news. He'd delighted in telling me every little detail, so I knew he was going to reassure her that everything would be okay, that there would be an explanation as to why I was late, and he was going to let her get right up to the entrance of the church. And then he was going to say that the reason he knew everything would be okay was because I'd given him a love letter to give to Tali when she arrived at the church..."

Becca's hand was now covering her mouth.

"And she will have opened it and seen my words. Saying I couldn't marry her. That I'd made a mistake. I didn't love her. That I hoped she realised she was better off without me anyway. Then he had her driven away from church and not a word was said about the why, only that I'd left her at the altar."

"B- but that's horrendous. I mean surely her friends must have wanted to kill you, her family? It would have been the ultimate humiliation."

"Everyone was asked to pretend I didn't exist, to just count it as a narrow escape from scum. I got dirty looks and a lot of people trying to find out why the wedding didn't happen. Tali never contacted me again. My belongings were boxed and sent to me. My clothes had been shredded." I smiled at that. "Couldn't blame her, but she left my important documents alone, and my bollocks."

Becca smiled at that. "I wouldn't have. You never talked to each other after, at all?"

"No. She took a job out of Willowfield. The first I heard she was back was when Brenda at the shop told me she was getting married again. I don't know if her wedding's here or somewhere else."

"Bloody hell, Callum. That's mental. How did your family handle it?"

"I called Milo when I knew it was too late for him to save the wedding. He got on the next train and met me. Phoned home and told them we'd be as long as we'd be. Got me up to date on everything that had happened. Him and Silas hadn't gone to the wedding, they'd turned over every stone they could to try to find me. We stayed in Edinburgh a week. I spent most of it drunk."

"Callum, her father shouldn't be able to get away with what he did." Becca's jaw was taut.

"Milo said the same; but like I told him, ultimately I knew Tali wanted her own babies, and this way she could have them. It wasn't that I didn't love her. I loved her so much I let her go find someone else. And now she has. She gets married again in a year's time."

"And how do you know she's truly happy?" Becca asked me.

"Because despite what I did to her, she's willing to attempt to walk up the aisle again."

"Yet she's not had kids." She said. "She wanted

children with you before the wedding. Why's she not done the same with this guy?"

"You're asking me questions that are not my concern."

"What if she never got over you? What if that's why? Because she's still hoping that you're going to turn up at her door and tell her you love her and not to marry him. Maybe she decided babies weren't everything if it meant you came back?"

"She's still better off with him than me. I'm damaged goods."

"Callum Waite, you are not—" the conversation went no further because there was a deafening noise as glass shattered, fragments coming towards us, and so near to Laurel who was asleep on the sofa, that afterwards our faces were pictures of abject horror. We turned to find a large brick lying on the carpet, a note attached to it with an elastic band.

I picked it up while Becca dived for her child, shielding her with her body.

"What does it say?" She asked me. I turned the note to show her. Written in thick black marker.

Leave, filthy Paedo wife.

A minute later the front door was banged on

making us both jump and then Violet's voice called out. "Becca. *Becca*, is everything okay?"

Carefully, dodging the glass, I moved to the front door and let Vi in. Her eyes searched past me towards the living room.

"Everyone's okay, just a little shaken. She's had a brick thrown through the window."

"Milo's gone running down the street, see if he can see anyone who might have done it."

"Fuck." If Milo caught them he'd probably slap them upside the head.

Violet walked into the living room and I followed her.

"Oh my god. Becca, are you okay?"

"We're fine, but that's it." Becca got to her feet, a sleepy Laurel in her arms. "This house is no longer our home. My daughter could have been seriously injured. What if that brick had hit her? I should have gone straight to my parents' instead of waiting until tomorrow."

Vi handed Becca her house key. "Go and settle Laurel down at ours and make yourself a drink or something. We'll get things straight here."

"The window." She said.

"House renovation services, remember?" I told her. "Milo and I will get it boarded tonight and then tomorrow we'll get the window replaced. Right now, do what Vi says and get next door."

Violet turned to me, an amused look on her face.

"What?"

"You sounded eerily like your older brother then."

Becca did as asked and left the house. I got the dustpan and brush that I was becoming all too familiar with and started to clear up the glass. After around fifteen minutes, Milo walked through the door.

"Anything?" I asked.

"Nope. Saw a couple of teens disappear towards the park dressed in the usual dark hoodies but no proof it was them. Been talking to Becca, making sure she's okay. Helped get Laurel settled."

Violet walked into Milo's arms and he kissed the top of her head. A pang of jealousy hit me for what they had together.

"You go back to Becca, Princess. She needs you more than me. Me and Cal will get the window boarded up and the house made safe."

And that's what we did. We worked together side by side, and as we did, I remembered the time

I'd spoken to Becca about Edinburgh and how my brother was my hero.

"Miley?"

"Yeah." He was checking the window board and didn't turn around.

"Just wanted to say that out of all of them, you're my favourite."

He turned round to me quickly. "You fucking dying, man?"

I laughed. "No. Just had a lot of things lately make me appreciate what I have. I'm so happy for you and Violet."

"You'll find your own princess, you know." He said, walking over and pulling me into a side hug.

"Maybe." I sighed.

"Or a prince if you continue with this growing a vagina emotion sharing." He bumped me away with his hip. "I reckon we're done here. In the house I mean." He started packing up. "Want to come back to ours for a beer?"

"Nah, you got enough going on. I'm heading home. See you tomorrow, probably."

I slipped out of the front door and cut through the side of Milo's, across the grass and back into our house. Jules was in the living room when I went to sit down.

"Where've you been? You missed your fave dinner. I left you a spare portion, but Finn ate it."

"I've eaten. I've been round at Becca's."

Her head tilted to the side. "Her electric go again?"

"Nope." I filled her in on Becca's breakdown, the Chinese, and the subsequent brick through the window. "So she's back at Vi and Milo's but tomorrow she's going back to her parents."

"Fuck, that woman has had it rough." Jules fiddled with a ring on her finger. "But I'm glad she's going back to her parents. I like her a lot, but she's not Milo's problem and she's not your problem either."

I opened my mouth to say something but didn't have any words to actually speak.

"Uh-oh."

"What?"

"You like her."

I gave a dismissive snort. "Don't be crazy. I just feel sorry for her. She just lost her husband."

Jules turned her body so she was completely facing me. "I didn't say you were about to profess your undying love to the woman. I'm well aware of her recent life event. I just know you, and I can tell that you like her." She placed her tongue over her teeth and sucked. “Deny it all you want. I ain’t fucking stupid.”

I ran a hand through my hair. “I don’t know what I feel. She’s a nice woman and she’s been dealt a shit hand in life and I know what that feels like. I don’t know if I like her or it’s just I feel sorry for her.”

Jules nodded.

“Angela was here when I came home earlier. She’d been talking to Dad. Eli is coming next Monday and staying until Friday. So if you can be around to help entertain our little brother that’d be cool.”

“Sure thing. He says he’s no good at DIY, but he can come hang with me at work a little.”

“He’ll like that. He’s so desperate to be a part of us, you know. A real part. Not to be the new kid, but to be one of the Waites.”

“But he’s not a Waite, is he? He’s a Dawson.”

“You know what I mean.”

"I do."

“I wonder where she is?” Juliet added quietly.

“Could be anywhere.” I took a seat at the side of her.

“Ezra could probably find her. He has the money to pay a PI.”

"I think we're better off not knowing, Jules. If she was interested, she'd have been in touch."

She sighed. "Yeah, you're right. We've been fine without her. We'll continue to be fine without her." She stood up. "I'm going to head up to my room and watch *The Stranger*. Catch you later, bro."

"Night, Jules. Love you."

She looked back at me with a bemused expression. "Love you, too, but don't tell the others I said that. Don't want them thinking I have a heart."

I laughed. My sister was so spiky on the surface, but we could all see that underneath there was a vulnerable abandoned daughter with trust issues.

Thinking of Ezra, I got out my phone and sent him a message.

Though you aren't here, we do miss you, bro. So don't leave it too long until you visit, okay? Eli's coming Monday but you'll always be one of the OG.

I was surprised when my phone pinged back more or less straightaway.

Ezra: Everything okay?

Yeah, just a neighbour lost her

husband. Makes you appreciate what you have more. And things are weird with Eli being around, brings up thoughts of where Mum went.

Ezra: I do miss you all. It's nothing personal my being away. I just love my job.

I know. Take care, brother.

Ezra: You too.

Switching on the television, I put it onto some mindless cop show and Dad, Callum, and Silas, eventually joined me. I didn't tell them all I loved them, but inside I thought how grateful I was that they were in my life, and how I hoped Becca managed to get the support she needed through the months and weeks ahead.

CHAPTER THIRTEEN

Becca

The next day, once I could escape Violet's mothering, or should I say smothering, I returned to my own house with Laurel. Luckily, the parties who had thrown a brick through the window had not returned. The living room was strangely dark because of the boarded-up window and so despite it being a bright, sunny day, I had to switch on the main light, conscious that I didn't want Laurel falling over, especially given that I hadn't had another chance to check for glass fragments on the floor. The first thing I did was set up Laurel's favourite DVD and leave her singing along while I did another thorough sweep of the floor. By nine am I had Milo and Josh Waite on my doorstep while a glazier's van parked up outside.

"Get a brew on then, Becca." Milo patted me on the back. I loved that he wasn't treating me any differently because I was a widow. He'd had pity in his eyes for me yesterday, but today he was back to his normal cheeky self.

He wandered up to Laurel and began dancing to the music of her DVD making her chuckle. She stood up grasping hold of his leg and trying to stop him while shouting, "No, Milo." She then proceeded to show him the proper dance and bless him he learned it until she was satisfied he could do it properly.

He turned to me, "That's some new moves to show Violet later," he winked. I laughed. "Bingo. That's what I've been missing, seeing that smile. Don't let the 'bleep' grind you down, Becca."

I simply nodded and walked into the kitchen to boil the kettle. Laurel had a tantrum at having to be moved away from her DVD, but I explained to her that Milo and Josh were mending the window and that she could watch them from the kitchen and help carry them a biscuit. Of course she kept eating the biscuits while keeping Milo and Josh thoroughly entertained by showcasing different dances or showing them her favourite toys. Despite my protests and attempts to keep Laurel in the kitchen, Milo and Josh said they didn't mind at all and it was nice to see a little one. Once an exhausted Laurel had been put down for a nap, I called the local estate agents and arranged for them to come and value the house. Given the appointment they gave me was for the following day, I called my parents and said it made sense for me to stay in Willowfield one further night and also gave me chance to do some packing. My intention once Laurel was awake again, was to go out and purchase some storage boxes, but Milo told me they had plenty of spare boxes back at the yard and he'd bring me some once he'd finished the window repairs.

By the afternoon, the window had been replaced, Josh had left, and Milo had gone and then returned with a lot of boxes. I then began packing away our belongings while Laurel found new things to play with, usually something I'd just that minute packed. I was so nervous that someone would come back to throw another brick through the window, so I made sure to keep Laurel away from them at all times.

I'd never realised how long it took to pack away

the simplest of items, but eventually I'd made a large inroads into packing up what Laurel and I could manage with at my parents' house, and had started packing away our other belongings ready for longer storage. There were certain items that held memories of Rob that I had no intention of taking with me into my future life. For these, I rang the charity shop who arranged to come and pick the items up the following day. After what had happened with the brick being thrown through the window, my mind was made up that it was time to sell this house and that though my future was uncertain, I knew for definite that Laurel and I no longer belonged here.

If someone had told me just two weeks ago, I would be having to sell my home as a widow of a liar and abuser, I would have thought they'd taken drugs. From being a woman who basically didn't have a care in the world, I now felt the weight of that world on my shoulders and I wondered how long it would be before I ever felt like the old Becca again, if ever.

After a final night at Violet and Milo's, Laurel and I went back to our house for what would be maybe the last time. The estate agent came, looked around the property and gave me a valuation that I accepted; and the charity came and picked up the items of furniture. I looked around at what was once my home and now was becoming a bare shell. I realised the house resembled me, once full of love and now pared back to an empty structure.

I was just about to call my father and ask him to come pick us up when there was a knock at the door. All knocks now made me jump in apprehension of what I might find at the other side of the door, so I was thankful when the peephole revealed Callum at the other side. I opened the door, stepped aside to let him pass and then closed it again firmly behind me after checking the street like some cheating mistress making sure no one had spotted my lover turning up.

"Wow, it looks so different in here with everything packed away." Callum said while his eyes roamed around the living room.

"I know, and it's so echoey. It makes Laurel's screeches seem twice as loud." I mimed putting my hand over my ears. Laurel herself was on the sofa playing with dolls and chattering away. She was so engrossed that she hadn't even stopped to say hello to Callum.

"I was just passing and I wondered if you'd have left yet. What time are you going?"

"Funnily enough, I was just about to call my dad and get him to come pick us up."

Callum looked at his feet, and then back up at me. "I know it's weird, Becca, and that we don't know each other well, but I wanted to just come and wish you all the best and to let you know that if you ever need me for anything, you have my number. I will always be at the other end of the line. No matter what time, day or night, you can ring me. I know you have your parents, but I remember when my life hit the skids, that sometimes I would have liked to be able to talk to someone outside of it all. To have someone who I could have just poured my heart out to without judgement. So if you need someone, you can call your friendly local electrician, okay?"

Emotion hit me as I realised that I really was leaving Willowfield behind. As tears began to fill my eyes, I stepped forward and Callum opened his arms and embraced me in a hug. We stood there for a few minutes while he let me cry, and then when I stepped back from his embrace, he walked into the kitchen, returning with some kitchen roll so I could blow my nose.

"Thank you, Callum Waite, for all your support, and please thank your family for everything they have done for me in the past couple of weeks. I seriously don't know what I would have done without you all. I'm moving away from Willowfield, but I'll still be in touch with Violet and Jules and so you never know, one day I might just turn up to a bowling night."

"That would be really nice, so let's not put a timeframe on it, but just say that it's not goodbye forever, it's just a goodbye for now, and that one day we might meet again." Callum said, and I could hear the emotion choking his voice.

"Callum, you need to talk to Tali. You need to tell her either the truth, or enough that you feel able to move on with your life and to start dating again. You're an amazing man and you will make a wonderful partner to some lucky woman out there. Don't close yourself off just because of your health issues. The right woman will be able to work around it. In fact, I want a promise from you right now, that by this time next week you'll have a date. I shall check with Violet that you've done it."

"You are so bossy."

"You're only just realising that?"

He chuckled and began to move towards the

door. As he passed Laurel, he tickled her under her chin. "Where are you going? You need to stay and have tea with me and my teddies." Laurel instructed him while picking up a teddy.

"Callum has to go now, sweetie."

Laurel pouted but then turned back to her teddies.

"If only we could all get over things so fast." I raised a brow at Callum.

I walked him to the front door, unlocked it, and watched as he began to walk down the path. As he reached halfway, he turned back around to face me and for a moment with the expression on his face, I wondered what he was going to say.

"By the way. While you're at your parents' house, if they have a bowling alley nearby, I'd get some practice in. Because when you come back to Willowfield, I intend to whoop your arse at bowling." He sniggered.

"In your dreams, Waite boy." I yelled back. "You just made that a challenge, and one thing you should know about me, I never back down from a challenge. So it's on. I don't know when, but one day I will return and when I do your arse is toast."

Callum walked off still smiling as he headed down the street, but he didn't look back. Closing the door, I called my father and I left Willowfield behind.

It was time for me to let my parents look after us in the way I'd always found suffocating, but this time I hoped would help me feel safe, until time had indeed had a chance to heal us, and I could think of what I did next.

CHAPTER FOURTEEN

Callum

Seeing the 'For Sale' sign appear at the entrance to Becca's house was strange. I didn't ask Violet if she'd heard from her because Becca had been right. I needed to speak to Tali. It would help me get some closure and then I needed to start dating again. So I couldn't have children biologically, but I could still be damn well more of a husband to someone than Rob had shown himself to be to Becca. Taking a deep breath, I knocked on Milo's door.

Violet answered. "Milo's not here, Cal. I've sent him out pricing up another job. I'm sure he'll not be much longer."

"Actually, it's you I've come to see." I shuffled from one foot to the other, because my mind was focused on talking to Violet, but my feet wanted to go in the opposite direction.

"Oh, sure, come in." She let me in and we walked into the living room. "Everything okay?"

I nodded, deciding to come straight out with it. "Vi, you know how you had counselling about your mum? How do you engage with a counsellor? Only, I need to talk to someone about the fact I can't have kids. It's stopping me from living my life. Somehow, I have to get past this and accept it."

A tentative smile appeared on Violet's lips. "That sounds like a wise decision, Callum. The worst thing about counselling is the fear of it, the fear of the process itself, and wondering what it will entail. Let me get us both a drink and we can chat about it and then if you're still sure you want to engage with one, I will grab you the number of mine. I had to pay privately because the counsellors on the NHS have incredibly long waiting lists."

Violet walked into the kitchen and I followed her through, taking a seat at her dining table and watching while she took two mugs out of the cupboard, put the kettle on, and grabbed a teabag for us both. “You having your usual?”

“Yes please.”

Having fixed our drinks, Violet came and sat on a chair at the side of me, after putting the mugs on the table along with an open packet of chocolate digestives.

“So what brought about the change in your thinking?”

“Becca really. We had a good chat about things before she left. She basically told me straight that I needed to sort myself out.”

Violet chuckled. “Yep, that sounds like Becca.” Her expression went thoughtful and she spoke to the air rather than making eye contact with me, “Gosh, I hope she manages to get some peace while she’s at her parents’ house. God only knows she deserves it.”

She looked back at me and I nodded.

“When I first went to counselling, I was so nervous. I didn’t know what the counsellor would look like, what her personality would be like, and whether she’d judge me for my actions. I almost didn’t go in, but I knew that I had to speak to someone and I didn’t want it to be anyone I knew. And that’s what happened. My counsellor turned out to be a really approachable person who guided me with questions, but sat and let me speak and listened to me without judgement. She got me to think about things and to realise that I was judging myself too harshly. The main thing was how she got me to see that there were no overnight miracles, but that I could work on myself slowly but surely until I felt like the real me again. She said something to me that will always stick in my mind and that was instead of trying to continually push up the hill in getting better, sometimes it was okay to rest at that exact spot on the hill and take time to gather yourself until you felt able to take another step upwards. What she said was so true because that's how I was, putting pressure on myself, thinking that because I'd lost my temper with my husband once, it would happen again and that I might turn into my mother with her violent temper. It has taken me a long time, Callum, to realise that this is extremely unlikely, but I don't think I'll ever forget the event that led me to the counsellor's door. I have coping strategies now and of course your bloody brother."

"Yeah, Milo is unlikely to let you have a downer on yourself seeing that he thinks the sun, moon, and stars shine out of your arse, alongside glitter and rainbows."

Violet rolled her eyes but the smile that kissed her lips showed her true feelings about my brother and cemented my feelings about going to see a counsellor. I wanted someone who thought of me and smiled in the same way.

"Thanks, Violet, for being so honest with me about your experience. I guess it's going to be difficult, especially as a guy, for me to go and pour out my thoughts and feelings to a stranger, but I need to do this. I need to be able to move on. I can't spend my life in the Waite family home while everyone meets the loves of their lives and moves out and I'm left knocking around the place with my dad."

"Hey, your dad will move on too. He's not going to stay single forever. We need to make sure we don't let him for a start. You're all grown up now and it's time Josh worked through his own issues and found some love outside of his family."

It was something I'd previously not given much thought to. I saw Dad as the constant; the person who was always there for us where our mother hadn't been. Even when we'd all started dating and our father gave us his advice, I'd not given a lot of thought to him dating again. I think we'd all pretty much accepted that Dad was bruised and broken after mum and happy to be on his own. That was the impression he'd always given us, but maybe we were wrong and that was just his way of masking his own problems. Perhaps he was sticking his head in the sand, distracting himself via his children when he should have been dealing with things and moving on himself. It seemed it was the Waite family way to pretend things hadn't happened and close yourself off from opportunities for happiness. Something that we all needed to change. With that in mind, I made up my mind once and for all that I would definitely make an appointment to see a counsellor.

I finished my drink, and then Violet got me the number of the woman she'd seen. She wrote it down for me on a scrap of paper and handed it to me. "If you need someone to go with you, to just sit in the car outside while you go in, I can do it. You just have to let me know when."

"Thanks, Violet." I said, followed by a grateful smile. "But I'll be okay. You never know, I might drag another one of the broken Waite family with me yet."

Violet's features softened. "Oh, Callum, you

aren't all broken, no more than anyone else. The rain pours down on us all at some time in our life. It's about how we deal with it. We can drown in it. We can put an umbrella up and try to pretend it's not even raining. We can dance in it regardless. All we can do is get wet and then slowly dry off."

"You're so wise, Violet Blake."

She smiled. "Right, I'd better get back to work now. Your Dad's been very flexible with me because of helping Becca, but she's gone now."

"Yeah, I'd better get to work too."

I left Violet's house clutching that piece of paper with the number of the counsellor on it, but more than that, I felt I was holding onto a small piece of hope for the future.

Before I went to work, I went back to our house, up to my room, and took my phone out of my pocket and dialled the number immediately. I knew if I didn't, I'd lose my confidence and make excuses as to why I shouldn't proceed. There was no time like the present and so I made an appointment to see Jennifer, the counsellor. The first appointment she had was for the following week. She explained that she worked at two different practices and that the only free appointment she had was at one an hour's drive away from Willowfield. I accepted it immediately, thinking that the drive would give me time to think both before the appointment and after it. Also, it meant that no one from Willowfield would be watching me enter the counselling practice and gossiping that it was no doubt to do with my ex-fiancee's upcoming wedding.

CHAPTER FIFTEEN

Callum

I was enjoying a beer on the back garden on Sunday afternoon when Milo came through the gate. He picked up the extra can I'd brought out in case I fancied another and plonked down onto the lounger at the other side of me.

"Doesn't matter how much you tan yourself, you'll always be an uglier version of me. Can't even take the advantages of being younger if you're going to age yourself through the sun. Hope you've got your factor fifty on there."

"Had a facial and waxed your bikini line, have you?" I quipped.

"You won't be laughing when I still look in my

twenties and people ask if you're my dad. I don't mind being in touch with my feminine side if it keeps me looking good. I have to keep Vi interested, you know." He held up his hands. "These get rough, so I've started using hand cream."

I groaned. "Was there a reason to this visit, other than you sharing skincare tips?"

"Yeah. So you know how me and Vi no longer have any secrets from each other?"

"Go on..." I braced myself for what was going to come out of his mouth because sometimes his advice was golden and sometimes he was like a cattle prod.

"So I know you're seeing a therapist. I won't tell anybody, mainly because if I do Vi's gonna cut my balls off and deny my penis any action; but I just wanted to say I'm glad."

"Thanks, bro. Good to have your support." I gave him a comradery smile. He was an idiot at times, but he always had my back.

"Yeah and also I want to marry Vi soon and need you as my best man if possible, or in attendance at least. Don't want you arriving and having post traumatic stress and screaming the place down or something."

Yep, idiot. I threw my now empty can at him, the last droplets landing on his chest.

"Steady on. I forgot to ask if this suncream was waterproof."

"I thought Violet wanted to wait to get married, given that you've been dating her a matter of weeks?"

He sighed. "I know. She's so bloody stubborn. She's stuck with me whether she likes it or not, so I don't know why she just doesn't give in. Do you know she suggested the summer of 2022? That's like two years away!"

"Give her some time, mate. Women like to plan stuff and do the whole dress, cake, venue, blah blah blah. I remember what Tali was like. She spent an hour deciding what kind of ribbon to have on the backs of the chairs at the reception. I mean, who the fuck cares? But they do. And the favours. You can't just put a chocolate on the table. It has to be a lottery ticket, or some kind of plant that blooms only on your anniversary and is named after the bride and groom. Then there's all the single-use cameras." I trailed off. "Actually, bro. Kidnap her and take her to Gretna Green or Vegas. Avoid all that crap."

Milo beamed. "See. I'll tell her you're on my side."

Blind panic must have hit my features because my brother guffawed and shoved me in the arm. "Your face."

"Don't do that to me. I don't want your fiancée as my enemy, because if she can keep you in line..."

"She mainly keeps me lying down."

I pretend heaved.

"So, after all this counselling, are you going to start dating again?" Milo's serious face was now in position.

"Yeah, time to get on with my life. Find a woman who'll put up with me. I figure if you've found one, there's definitely someone out there for me."

We sat chatting for a few more minutes and then we heard the doorbell ring.

"Wonder who that is?" My brow furrowed. We didn't get many visitors on a Sunday afternoon. No one came to fetch us, so I presumed it was a door-to-door salesperson and Milo and I carried on talking about football and how terrible our local team were playing.

The clatter of high-heeled shoes came from

behind and a female voice went, “Hello, boys,” in a sultry accent.

As I spun my head around to look at our visitor, Milo clapped his hands and once again that guffaw exploded from him.

“Fucking hell, brill.”

The woman’s smile dropped, and she began scowling. “Why are you laughing?” She said haughtily.

“Ezra, I’d recognise those fucking knock knees anywhere. I don’t care how good the rest of your prosthetics are, they need to stick some shit on your knees.” Milo pointed.

“Oh fuck off,” our elder brother said as he dropped his female accent and his ‘actor’ accent and fell straight back into being a Waite brother. He kicked his heels off and walked barefoot over to us. “Those things are evil. Why women wear them I don’t know.”

We both stood up and hugged our brother in turn.

“Do not get that shit on my face.” Milo pointed to Ezra’s lips. “My woman will smack me first, ask questions later.”

“I’m looking forward to meeting her.” Ezra said. “I’ve access to psychologists for her, to test her mental state at living with you and accepting your proposal."

Milo placed his hands on his hips and his legs wide apart. "She's already done that, big bro, so ner-ner na ner-ner."

There was something about when any number of us got together, that we dropped back into being childlike. It usually resulted in someone having their head rubbed with knuckles.

"You never said you were coming." I chastised my brother, although good-naturedly.

"And spoil the surprise!" He sat himself down on Milo's lounger. "Get us a beer, Miley."

Milo chuntered but walked off through the gate towards his own house.

"So how long are you here for?" I asked Ezra, though it was weird seeing as he looked like someone else entirely and not even the right sex.

"About a week in London filming. I start Wednesday and will need to travel down Tuesday. So, I'm only here a couple of days, but I thought I could meet Eli. Be good to not be a stranger to him."

"He's coming to stay tomorrow until Friday, so he'll love it."

"That works out perfectly then. Obviously, I'll

try to surface at a reasonable time in the morning, but I'm five hours behind you, so wake me up if I'm dead to the world. Don't tell him I'm here either. It'll be a nice surprise for him."

"God, he'll be starstruck. He can't believe he has a famous actor for a brother."

Ezra laughed. "So, if Eli's coming then he'll be in Milo's old room, right?"

"Yeah, Finn has it all set up for him."

"I'll see if I can stay in Milo's spare room then."

"Nah, your family will want to see you. You can take my room and I'll sleep on the sofa for a couple of nights. It won't hurt. Can't have your delicate acting skin damaged by sofa surfing. I'll make sure to order some thousand percent Egyptian cotton sheets."

Ezra stuck out his tongue at me.

"How come you're not staying in a hotel like usual?"

He shrugged. "I don't know. Maybe it's something to do with the whole Eli sitch. I just feel like if Dad can accept Eli then I shouldn't carry on being an arse pain to him. Should try to smooth things over."

"So you're no longer blaming Dad for Mum

leaving now you can see she has form?" I arched a brow.

"Ouch, those words were a bit barbed, but yeah, something along those lines."

"I think having Eli around is helping Dad to deal with things a little. Angela helps."

"Angela? Is he dating?"

"God, no. Angela is Eli's mum. She's been there since he was a baby. Put up with his dad's behaviour it would appear, to make sure Elijah had someone."

"Good job really, because otherwise goodness knows how the kid would have ended up, with an absent mother and junkie father."

"Exactly. Anyway, I think Dad speaks to her regularly on the phone, only she's very protective of Eli and I think she's nervous that she might lose him, given that she's not a blood relation." I laid my head back on my own lounger and placed my hand across my eyes to block out the sun.

"I wonder where she is?" I stated.

"I take it you mean our errant mother." Ezra replied.

"Yup. She could be anywhere in the world. She could even be dead."

Ezra snorted at that. "You're so dramatic.

Thought of writing for Hollywood?"

I took my hand away from my face and squinted over at him. "She could be. Violet didn't know Dan was dead."

"Dan was a weak-arsed junkie. Our mother was strong enough to walk out on six children."

"Seven."

"Fuck, yeah, seven."

"There could even be more. Who knows if she did it again?"

"Some people weren't meant to be parents." He said bitterly. I flinched, but of course Ezra didn't know I couldn't have children. His words weren't meant for me.

Milo came back to the gate, Vi behind him. I realised he'd been a long time in getting Ezra a drink and decided to wind him up about it.

"That drink was a long time coming, did something else *come up*?" I winked.

Milo scowled as he came closer. "Did it hell. I've had to wait while she's got changed and done her hair and make up." He kept his voice low near my ear while Violet introduced herself to Ezra like she'd just met the Queen.

"Look, she's even got a copy of a bloody women's magazine he was on." He grumbled, as we watched Vi shake the magazine and pen she was holding in Ezra's face.

"You don't think she accepted my proposal just to get near him, do you?" He asked, showing an air of vulnerability seldom seen in my brother.

"Don't be ridiculous. She's just fangirling. Let her have this moment, because soon she'll get to know the real Ezra and the starry eyes will disappear. He'll just become another member of the Waite family to her. He farts like the rest of us."

"So are we all going to go down the pub later?" I shouted across to Ezra. "Let the local superstar have his moment."

"I'll go looking like this." He pointed to his face. "Then I'll be left in peace."

"Yeah, right, as if Geoff won't have you covered." I laughed.

"Go and get that crap off your face and spend some more time in the house with Dad, Finn, Silas, and Jules." Milo said bossily.

"Noooooo. They can come to the pub later as well, can't they?" Violet pouted. "I'm chatting to Ezra right now."

Milo huffed through his nose. It was audible to me, but not to the still starstruck Violet.

He left it for a further few minutes and then he

told me he'd see me later, went up to Violet, kissed her cheek and went back into the house. Ten seconds later I saw Ezra and Violet looking extremely uncomfortable before she yelled, "That fucking man."

She went stomping off in the direction of her house and I looked questioningly at Ezra. "Milo farted," was his simple response.

I needed to be careful what I said to Milo. It obviously gave him ideas.

Ezra did clean all the make-up off his face before we went to the pub. Jules told him straight that she wouldn't be able to take it if people declared him the prettiest Waite. She provided him with a pack of cleansing wipes and told him to hurry up.

Eventually, everyone was ready to go, and we walked en masse down the road and around the corner to the Half Moon pub. As we walked through the door, the landlord, Geoff, spotted Ezra and banged the gong that usually heralded last orders, making a few customers double check their watches and another couple stand up quickly to head to the bar. As everyone went quiet wondering why Geoff had signalled last orders at eight thirty at night, he clapped his hands together as we approached and began to shout, "Well, well, well, if it isn't Willowfield's golden boy Ezra Waite, returned from the Big Apple and La La land, now back where he belongs." As Geoff beckoned him over and asked him what he wanted to drink on the house, a low hum of chatter travelled around the bar. Some of the patrons, the regulars on a Sunday night, knew that Ezra Waite was the local boy done good and smiled at him or walked over and patted him on the back. The Willowfield regulars did not treat Ezra with any starry eyes or special treatment. Neither did they expect him to get his hand in his pocket and buy them all a drink. In fact, it was the reverse. They all wanted to buy him a drink to let him know they weren't after his riches. The landlord banged his gong again and shouted at the top of his voice, "Anyone caught annoying Ezra for an autograph tonight or taking photos of him will find themselves barred from the pub. Leave the lad alone with his family and let him enjoy a night of peace in his hometown." The regulars clapped, cheered, and whooped as we walked over to one of the larger tables and then carried on with their evening like we hadn't come in at all.

"How come Ezra always gets a free pint when

he's stinking rich, but those of us who have to graft hard for every penny have to bloody buy theirs." Moaned Finn.

"I have to graft bloody hard too." Ezra picked up a beer mat and flung it towards Finn. "I've been wearing four-inch heels all week while being on a film set from five am until one am."

I noticed that Violet was sitting watching the interaction between the brothers with silent rapture, while Milo sat with his arms folded across his chest, pouting like a child who'd just been denied an ice cream.

"That barmaid, Lisa, keeps looking over here, Callum." Milo stated, his eyes meeting mine. Ezra's head quickly turned to look at me.

"Lisa?"

Milo nodded. "Callum asked her out the other week. Well, he meant to ask her out, but instead, he ended up giving her a business card and himself a headache."

"Leave me alone. I told you I need practice. It's been a long time since I dated anyone and I clearly forgot how to talk to women." I raised my hands at him in a gesture of surrender.

"So she didn't agree to go out with you then?" Ezra queried.

"No, I honestly don't think she even realised I was trying to ask her out."

Milo looked back to the bar area where Lisa's gaze flickered over in our direction before her attention had to return to serving a customer.

"Yup, definitely looking over with interest. You might want to try asking her out again. Only this time try it in English rather than nervous gibberish." Milo advised helpfully. "What do you think, Silas? You're the one who knows how to woo the ladies." He shouted across to Silas. Silas had been chatting with Jules and was oblivious to my conversation, so Milo filled him in on my desperately lacking chat up skills and explained once again how he wanted the expert's advice. Of course Silas lapped up the compliment.

"Look, Callum, you just need to go over there, tell her she looks lovely tonight and then ask her if you can ring her sometime to arrange a date."

"That's what was supposed to happen last time, but he almost ended up testing her electrics instead of her mattress." Milo quipped.

Violet elbowed Milo in his arm. "Leave him alone, Milo Waite. Your own chat up lines leave a lot to be desired. They belong more to a Carry On film than they do the 21st century."

"You fucking love it, Princess."

As Violet rolled her eyes at him, Milo stood up, picked her up, and put her over his shoulder.

“Say goodnight to everyone, Princess.”

“Put me down, you brute.” She cried, banging her fists on his back.

“Goodnight all. I’m off to remind my woman how much she loves my c—”

“The next words out of your mouth better be ‘caveman ways’, Milo Waite.” Violet yelled.

He laughed wickedly and then walked out of the pub still carrying her over his shoulder.

"So who is betting that Violet will be back here within five minutes, followed by a red cheeked Milo?" Jules asked with a raised brow.

"No, she digs it really." I turned towards my sister. "I have been watching them closely lately and they really are just madly in love with each other, warts and all."

“It’s good at least one of us has managed to find someone.” Ezra exhaled a deep sigh.

“So you’re not hiding anyone in the Big Apple then?” I asked him.

His eyes widened and for a moment he looked uncomfortable and I recalled the female voice I’d heard in the background when I’d called him about

Eli. But then his face became composed and he shook his head, another sigh leaving his mouth.

"No. There's no secret love of my life in New York."

When I had enjoyed a couple more pints that my siblings brought to the table, I finally got up the courage to go to the bar and attempt to ask Lisa on a date once more. She might well say no, but I needed to practice anyway. Plus, I'd kept looking over at her and on more than one occasion—several in fact—she'd been looking back over at me. Feeling brave, I approached the bar.

"Hey, Lisa. How are you?" *Way to go, Callum. Bowl her over with your amazing repertoire, why don't you?* I thought sarcastically. It was better that I treated this like pulling off a plaster. "Do you fancy going out one night, for a drink?" I looked at her face with its hesitant features and then I realised what I had said. "God, of course you don't want to go out for a drink; not when you spend your time serving them to other people. How about dinner instead?"

She smiled at me which put me more at ease. "It must be nice to have Ezra home. Is he staying long? Only won't you want to spend time with him?"

What a thoughtful person, I acknowledged, while my mind wondered if she was giving me the brush off again. "Oh, he's only here for two days. He goes to London on Wednesday. So if you fancy that meal on Wednesday evening, Ezra will have left."

"Wednesday evening it is then." Lisa said and then she peeled the covering paper off a beer mat, picked up a pen and scrolled her phone number across the mat before picking it up and handing it to me. "Send me a text to let me know the details." She added. "Now if you'll excuse me, I'd better get back to work."

I returned to my seat with a huge smile on my face. Ezra looked at me as if I was under a microscope. "So you went to the bar to get me a drink but came back empty-handed." He raised a brow, "care to explain?"

"I have a fucking date, bro." I sat back in my seat, my heart beating fast with the adrenaline rush of having taken a chance for once in my life.

"With Lisa?" My brother checked.

I nodded.

"Interesting." He added. “Well done, bro. Now is it a pint you want because I’d better go to the bar?”

CHAPTER SIXTEEN

Callum

Ezra's visit was like a breath of fresh air. All of us were so happy to have him in the house again. He and Dad talked alone for a time and the tension that had been in the house when he'd visited before disappeared. Eli came to stay and was like an overenthusiastic puppy at having his famous brother in the house.

But before we knew it, it was Tuesday and time for Ezra to go on to London.

"Will you get chance to come back to visit us before you return to New York?" Eli asked him, a pang in his tone.

Ezra rubbed the hair on the top of Eli's head.

"Not this time, squirt. But I'll be back in a few months for a premiere and I'll make sure to see you then. You still want to come to one, right?"

"Fuck, yeah." Eli asked. Then he sensed my eyes on him and looked to see my raised brows.

"Erm, sorry. Yeah, I can't wait. Will I need a suit?"

"We'll sort all that nearer the time." Ezra told him. "In the meantime, concentrate on school and keeping your mum sweet."

And then with hugs for us all, something vastly different to the usual Ezra, his taxi arrived and he left.

"Do you reckon he's fucking dying?" Milo asked. "Cos he's hugging us like he cares. Best acting of his life."

"I reckon he's dropping his mask." Dad told Milo. "We had a good chat. What your mum did with Eli has made him realise that he couldn't carry on blaming me. That your mother has form for abandoning her children. We might just have Ezra back." I turned to see a tear in my dad's eyes.

We all stepped forward and had a massive family hug. And then dad reminded us there was work to be done.

I took Eli around with me on my jobs. Despite

saying he was useless at practical stuff, he soon learned how to make a good cup of tea and began asking lots of questions. His interest in what I was doing was genuine and I found myself enjoying explaining things to him. I realised that while I might never be a father, I could be a good male role model to Eli, take him under my wing a bit, and encourage him to make the right choices in life. Suddenly, a cloud in my life seemed to have lifted. There was purpose in caring for my brother, and then I had a date tomorrow night. Finally, I saw a way forward.

Before I knew it, the time had arrived. I was putting on a shirt and a pair of slacks and going on a date. I thought it would be Milo riding my arse about it but instead Finn was on my case.

"You got condoms?" He caught me on the upstairs landing just as I left my room to walk down the stairs.

I tilted my head and then shook it at him in disbelief. "I'm not putting out on a first date."

"Such high standards for someone whose right bicep is twice the size of his left."

"Sod off."

He patted me on the back. "Seriously, bro. It's

good to see you getting back on the horse, and Lisa's a nice looking filly."

"Spend less time with Miley." I ordered him and he just laughed. "What about you, anyway? Seeing anyone at the moment?"

"Nope. I have a friends-with-benefits situation and that suits me just fine." He replied.

I said I'd see him later and with that I was out of the door, into the car and picking up Lisa from outside her house.

"Hey," she said as she climbed into the passenger seat.

"Hi. I booked us a table at Bella Italia. Is that okay?"

"Absolutely. I'm craving a pizza so that will hit the spot." She rubbed at her tummy. Lisa was attractive with freckles across her cheeks and I liked the fact that as she patted her stomach it wasn't washboard flat. Silas liked the fit types. I preferred someone who'd rather sit with a large popcorn and watch a film. I hoped Lisa was like that.

"So did Ezra get off okay?" She asked me as I drove to the restaurant. I liked that she'd remembered what I said about him going, but then again, I'd said for us to meet today because he'd have left.

Stop trying to make her fit your boxes, I chastised myself. *Relax and let it come naturally*.

"Yep, that's him off to London filming and he doesn't have time to come back for now. He says he'll be back in a few months when he has a premiere."

"Living his best life, yeah?" Lisa said sighing.

"Yeah, makes our lives seem a little mundane, doesn't it? But do you know, I wouldn't swap him for the world."

"Really, how come?"

"Because he doesn't live a 'normal' life. He doesn't know who to trust. Most of the people around him want him for what he can do for them."

"Why doesn't he come home then? You'd think he'd realise he has more to be here for than there."

"Quite simply, he loves what he does. He shrugs off the movers and shakers, does his job and then goes home. He says he's not dating but I heard a female voice when I last spoke to him in the background. I think he is, but he's always been very private."

Lisa nodded. "So can I ask something personal, straight off?"

I tapped the steering wheel as we'd come to a red traffic light. "Sure?"

"You asking me out. Is it because your ex is getting married? I heard the news on the grapevine. I know the rumours are that you left her at the altar and haven't dated properly since."

"Yes and no." I answered truthfully, as I looked around the corner and turned into the restaurant car park. "No, not just because she's getting married. I'm happy for her, but yes in that it was another factor in me realising I had to move on and start dating again."

"Yes, at some point you realise you have to just get on and live your life, don't you?"

I pulled up and turned the engine off before getting out of the car. I was going to walk around to let Lisa out, but she was already out of the car before I got there.

We checked in at the entrance and were shown to our seats by a waitress who handed us menus, took our drinks orders and said she'd be back in a few minutes to take our food orders.

"So what's your own dating history?" I asked her. "I'm guessing nothing noteworthy or the whole of Willowfield would already know about it."

She moved her fringe out of her face and

looked at me. "Long term on and off boyfriend who then became an off. I was engaged for a while to a guy I dated for a year before that ended, and a few regular dates and never to be repeated dates in between."

"Still looking for Mr Right then?"

"Something like that." She laughed.

The waiter came with a coke for me and a glass of red wine for Lisa.

We carried on chatting and ate some lovely food. It was a nice evening, but there was no spark between us. At times there were awkward silences where we then smiled and made up things to talk about. She refused a dessert and I realised that the date was over, and my relief showed me that there wouldn't be a second one.

I asked for the bill which Lisa insisted on going halves on. I wasn't happy but she wouldn't have it any other way.

As we walked out of the restaurant, I touched her arm and pulled her to face me gently. "Thanks for tonight, Lisa. My first date after, well, my past, was always going to be difficult, and now it's done. It was a nice night, but I know we're just friends."

Her face relaxed. "Shit, I thought you were

going to try to kiss me then and I'd got to push you away."

I laughed. "I didn't think I was that revolting."

She laughed back. "You're not. You'll make someone a lovely boyfriend. Just not me. But I also had a nice night. Friends, yeah?"

I made a dramatic, sweeping, 'head to my forehead' gesture. "Friend-zoned. Way to destroy my self-esteem."

She playfully punched me in the arm. "Behave."

"Come on, let me take you home."

"Thanks." She got back in the car. I drove back to her house and then once again thanked her for a nice night. I watched her walk to her doorway, and she gave me a small wave before going inside and closing the door.

As I drove back to mine, I expected disappointment to hit, but instead relief flooded through me. Relief that I'd survived a date and could see myself dating again.

Finn was still around as I walked back into the house. He looked at his watch. "It's only half-past ten. What are you doing back at this time?"

I smiled. "Nothing happening between us.

Pleasant enough evening, but we both agreed we're nothing more than friends."

"And you're smiling about that? You're a weirdo. I've already explained my own situation. You can be friends-with-benefits."

"Nah, it's not for me. Not with Lisa anyway. I think I know now that I just picked Lisa because she was pretty, single, and well, there in front of me: as in, in the pub. We didn't have a connection. However," I emphasised the word dramatically. "My first date in forever is out of the way and now I finally feel I can move on and get back to it. Have a little fun." I wiggled my eyebrows.

"Good on you. Fancy a beer?" Finn asked me. The door opened and Eli came through with Silas, Jules, and Dad. They'd been to the cinema. We all sat in the living room together for a while before people made their way to bed. As I sat with them, I felt blessed at the family I had around me.

I was on a job the next morning when a text came through from Milo.

House next door sold. Wonder who the new neighbour will be? If he's good

looking can you help me rearrange his face... jk.

I wasn't expecting my reaction to his text to be so visceral. A sinking feeling hit my stomach as I read and reread the message. That was it. Becca was gone. I'd only known her a short time, but it had been enough to make a lasting impression. I hoped now she could move on with her and Laurel's life. I got in my van ready to arrange my work for the day and drove past her house, wanting to see the sign for myself. There it was. An empty house and a SOLD sign.

Driving into the yard, I left the van and walked into the office where Violet manned the reception for our renovation business. As usual Rocky leapt up at me as I walked in. He was a gorgeous little thing. I might have to get myself a dog one day. It was time to think of new beginnings.

"Morning, Cal. Want a brew seeing as your first job's not for a while yet?"

"Why not?"

She went into the kitchen to make drinks and I carried on fussing the Staffy at my feet. "Here you go." She placed the drink down on the table in front of me. "So how was the date?"

"Friend-zoned. On both sides. But I've started

getting myself back out there, haven't I? It wasn't a total waste."

"I think it's great. Now just keep going."

"I'm starting to think about everything, you know? Don't tell Milo because this is just me thinking outside the box, but the whole 'sold' sign situation today on Becca's made me think about getting my own place sometime. Not right now because I don't want to rush things, but I thought this is stuff I can discuss at my counselling appointment. Maybe not tomorrow's but at a future one. Can think about properly moving on with my life. I wouldn't want to be too far away because I want to see everyone regularly, especially with Eli, but..." I shrugged. "God, I'm rambling on, sorry."

Violet smiled and lifting her mug took a drink of her tea. "Cal, this is fantastic. You've obviously been avoiding living your life, and now, no matter what sparked this, you're starting to think of the future. Now, personally, I can't say don't rush things because, hey, Milo, but do whatever feels comfortable. Talking things over will help so much, Cal. It really will, but like I've said to you before, I am always here to listen."

"Thanks, Violet. I'm glad Milo decided to claim you for his own because you're a welcome addition to the family. Oh and a heads up, he's on a mission for your wedding to happen sooner rather than later. He completely got the wrong surname in life, that man."

"Yes, well Milo needs to be taught about patience and so he can caveman all he likes, but this is one mission he's not winning."

"Have you heard anything from Becca?" I asked.

"No. I sent her a text, but she's not replied yet. Maybe she won't?"

"I'm sure she will. You've been such a good friend to her. She's probably just finding her feet at her parents' house."

"Yeah, you're probably right."

I drank up my cuppa. "Thanks for the drink and the chat. I'm off to my first job, and then I'll be back to the house to drag the teenager out of bed and round with me for the afternoon."

Violet nodded and then standing up, she walked over and hugged me. "You'll be fine, Cal. All you need is to take it one step at a time."

And I believed her. I actually thought that at some point in the future, my life might turn out okay after all. I just had to try living it.

CHAPTER SEVENTEEN

Becca

For once my parents' fussing didn't bother me at all. Having more of our own things with us, like my favourite throw to snuggle up under at night, and Laurel's huge array of toys, made it feel less like we were a burden and more like we belonged. With my mother's Kenyan heritage, she had never understood my need to be so independent, forever telling me that it took many people to raise a child successfully. I didn't tell her that it was the fact that our own house when I was growing up was always so full of family and friends, with hardly ever a minute to ourselves, that made me want to move out at the earliest opportunity to get some longed for peace and quiet. But maybe my mother had a point, that you couldn't do everything yourself.

The last few weeks had shown me that, as my next-door-neighbours and the family across the garden had included me like I was one of their own despite not really knowing me. Taking care of me in my hour of need. And now it was time to let my mum do her thing, so I could expect to catch up with lots of family and friends while I was here. My father just kept quiet in the background and let her get on with it.

I'd been here for almost two weeks now and after making enquiries at the local nursery, it was Monday lunchtime and time to take Laurel to a new place to socialise, where she could hopefully make new friends without the stigma of her father's behaviour sticking to her like a hair suit. Lord knows, she needed to go somewhere to work off some of the extreme energy fizzing around in her little body as she dashed around my parents' living room almost knocking her granny over in the process.

"Come on, sweetie. Let's go play at your new nursery." I stood up after fastening her shoes, picked up her coat and said goodbye to my mum and dad. The nursery was about a fifteen minute walk away for little legs and I looked forward to the fresh air.

"Kaa chonjo," Mum said as I opened the door. *Be alert.* I turned back to her and nodded my head. "Always, Mama."

She'd said it all my life, but nothing could have warned me about my husband, and now I felt I'd be on high alert for the rest of my life.

After introducing Laurel to her nursery teacher, she immediately went running over to the dress-up section and started chatting to two other little girls. "Not shy then?" The teacher, Mrs Lattimer exchanged a knowing look with me, that was no doubt borne of meeting lots of small children over the years and working out a personality within a few seconds. "Nope, and a chatterbox, so good luck at getting her to not talk through story time. My tip, ask her to mime the story for the other children. That way she can still wriggle but at least everyone can hear you."

"She sounds a lot of fun."

I nodded while looking back at the best thing I ever achieved in my life. "She's amazing. Exhausting, but amazing."

"Well you leave her with me for the afternoon

and go and grab a hot drink and put your feet up. You said you're staying with your parents for the time being while your house sells?"

"Yeah, so the putting my feet up might not be an option. My mum will no doubt have me earning my keep."

With a smile and a last look back at Laurel, who couldn't give two hoots that this was the first time she'd been there other than when we'd visited two days ago, I left and walked back to the house where I found a note from my mum saying she'd gone to a friend's house and that I did in fact have the house to myself. I didn't hesitate to grab a book, a hot drink, and make the most of the few hours I had until I had to walk back for Laurel again.

By the time I went to collect Laurel from nursery again, Mrs Lattimer knew that her daddy had died and was in heaven. Actually, if heaven and hell were real, I didn't think he'd be in heaven at all, but it still helped to explain things to Laurel if she could look up at the sky and 'talk to Daddy'. As Mrs Lattimer gave me her condolences, some of the other parents collecting their children overheard and I could see passing looks of sympathy on their faces. I realised that here I could properly mourn my husband, the husband I had known and loved. Not the person he'd turned out to be, but the one I'd had in my life for six years. Over the next few days, I got into mundane conversations with a few of the regular attending mothers and soon they were asking me about what they'd overheard. A new path started to appear before me. New mums with kids who didn't know our past, a new way forward. Yet always in the back of my mind was the truth, and I wondered if I'd ever be able to find a way to accept both parts of Rob as a whole.

Violet had left me alone for a few days to settle in which I was grateful for. I didn't want to have to keep updating people on my life. I needed that time out and Violet seemed to understand. When I'd left, she'd just said for me to keep in touch at my own pace.

On the Friday afternoon, over two weeks after I'd moved into my parents' house, I sent her a text.

Becca:Hey! Hope all okay. Laurel has loved her first week at nursery. If everything continues as well, then I think I might look for a rental around the area. I don't want to put firm roots down anywhere for a while but having Laurel near my parents is a good thing.

I soon received a reply.

Violet:Hey back at you. Good to hear you're doing okay. All fine here. Your house is fine. Glad you are surviving being around the parents. Have you heard from Rob's mum?

Becca:No. It's her loss. She hardly saw Laurel anyway, so I doubt she'll miss her.

Violet: Sorry, you sent me a quick text and I'm already asking you awkward questions...

Becca:It's fine. Here they believe I'm a proper widow and that's how I'm being treated. I can grieve. Which is good. I lost an amazing husband and I need to grieve for him.

Violet:You do.

Becca:I just don't know what to do about the part of me that hates him.

Violet: Give it time. Let me give you the number of the counsellor I saw. You don't have to use it, but it's there if you need it. If you need someone to talk to.

She sent me the number. Maybe one day in the

future I might need to talk to someone if time didn't make my head accept everything, but I didn't want it now. For now, I needed simple. Take Laurel to nursery, come home, be with family, simple.

Becca:Thanks. Love to Milo and of course to Rocky. I'll message you again in a couple of weeks or so, and then you'll have to come over here for a girls night!

Violet:Sounds like a plan! Take care of you and Laurel. Miss you xoxo

Becca: Miss you too.

And it was true. I missed Violet's kind nature, Milo's cheeky and bossy ways, Callum's kindness, Jules' take no bullshit tone, Josh's protectiveness. The Waite family were a lovely family. They just weren't mine.

Putting my phone away, I went to help prepare the evening dinner, after which I planned a nice long soak in the tub while granny and grandpa watched over Laurel.

As I enjoyed a leisurely soak, I started to see the benefits of having grandparents nearby. I would definitely make sure that any new place was in kidsitting distance. After wrapping myself in my robe and putting a towel turban style on my head, I made my way back downstairs to grab a glass of water before I started Laurel's bedtime routine.

My mum and dad were giggling as I walked into the room, and Laurel was looking at them with a mischievous look on her face as she giggled back. "I don't know where you got her from." My dad quipped. "She belongs on the stage." He looked back at Laurel. "Show, Mummy. Do it again."

Laurel picked up the Barbie and Ken dolls in her hands. She jumped Ken across the floor towards Barbie. "Give us a kiss, Princess." She said in a deep, gruff voice.

My mum and dad laughed again. "That voice." My dad said. "It's creasing me up. She sounds like she's on forty-a-day! You need to get her into a drama club when she's old enough." They weren't aware that my daughter had obviously spent far too much time listening to Milo Waite. Seemed I wasn't the only one who that family had made an impression on.

CHAPTER EIGHTEEN

SIX MONTHS LATER

Becca

It had been six months. Six months since I had said goodbye to the house that used to be my home. Six months since I had put that house up for sale, and six months since I had had any contact with Violet or any of the Waite family. The house had sold quickly to a cash buyer. Though I had been in no big rush to look for a new home, after a couple of months of living with my parents, I realised it would be better for Laurel, my parents, and my sanity if we got a place of our own. At first, I had thought about renting, but as a house I'd admired on the walk to school came up for sale, I took it as a sign and made an offer. As a cash buyer myself with no chain they'd accepted my offer almost immediately.

The two bedroomed house was small—smaller than our previous home—but then I'd had a lot less budget for this house.

The girls who had suffered at the hands of my husband had decided to pursue his estate in court. For mine and Laurel's peace, I had reached out through a solicitor and told them that they could share fifty per cent of what the house had sold for between them and that if they wished for more than they could pursue it through the courts. I was assured that it was doubtful that a court would make me pay anything out of my own pocket and that they would think I was being generous in not taking a portion of the proceeds for our daughter. In fact, it would be likely that the recompense they were seeking would be swallowed up in legal fees. I made sure they signed a contract that protected my daughter, although I hated silencing the mouths of Rob's victims. But my daughter was also a victim in this, and I needed to ensure that anything she learned about her daddy came from me.

Rob's mother was appalled at my actions and

told me that she still believed that the girls were liars, ironic given how she'd behaved when she thought Zoey might be pregnant. She chose to have nothing more to do with me and Laurel. As far as I was concerned, if she wanted to see her granddaughter she could, but she would have to reach out to me now. I was done trying to be the peacemaker with the carnage Rob left behind. From now on, my daughter's happiness and my own future life were my priority, and if we never saw Paula again then so be it.

I'd changed my surname when I first returned to my parents' house and changed my daughter's too. I was not a Staveley and my daughter would be one biologically only. Laurel was so young she hadn't noticed the change.

It had taken me a long time to get to the stage where I had some kind of peace and that was in no small part due to the counsellor Violet had given me the details for, and whose support I'd eventually sought.

I'd been through so many emotions over the past months, but Jennifer had helped me realise that I wasn't to blame for anything Rob had done and so I shouldn't punish myself. I was allowed to mourn the man I believed I had been married to, but also I didn't have to feel guilty that my mourning was less, that I'd moved on faster than I'd have expected to, because of the ugly truths that had come to light.

Last week I'd actually been out for a coffee with one of the single dads at Laurel's nursery. It was only a friend thing, but I knew I wouldn't rule out finding happiness again now, although I did know my trust would be hard won. I'd stopped thinking about the future in the longer term. The past months had shown me that nothing was certain in this life and that life could change in the blink of an eye, so I was all for living in the moment. And the current moment was that it was February of a brand new year and Laurel and I had been in our new home for ten days now.

Not much needed doing to it, which I was thankful for because I could wield a paintbrush no problem, but there was no way I could have coped with a renovation project like Vi's had been.

Vi. A hit of guilt flooded my stomach. At first, I'd kept in touch, but as I settled into my new life here in Hill Green, it seemed more sensible for me to stick with the new and let go of any ties to my old life.

But now I felt guilty because Vi had been a good friend and after a while I'd just let her texts go unanswered until they stopped appearing. The last one had simply said.

This is my last text. I don't know if you lost your phone or have made the decision to move on, but I am ALWAYS here. Even if it's five years from now. V xo

Once again, I hesitated, wondering if I should send a quick text, just to let her know how I was getting on. But once more, I decided against it. What was the point? I had no intention of ever going back to Willowfield. No, it was best I just moved on.

The only thing in my new house was I could use a few more sockets around the place. It would be so simple to ring Callum Waite and ask him to help; but, *come on, Becca,* I scolded myself, there would be loads of electricians much closer to home.

I thought about Callum from time to time. Wondered if he'd ever managed to speak to his ex, and whether he was back dating again.

No one was more surprised than me when I walked out of my counsellor's offices to find Callum walking in, his tool bag in his hand.

"Cal."

"Becca."

We both spoke at the same time.

Cal scrubbed a hand through his hair. "Erm, it's good to see you, even if we are stood outside..." He trailed off.

"Well, I can see you're here for work, whereas, yes I'm here for my issues. Though that was actually my last session."

"Well, I'm here to do a job today, but actually I came here myself. Vi gave me Jennifer's number. I had six weeks of appointments about my own... issues."

"Surprised I haven't bumped into you before then. Well..."

"Do you want to go grab some lunch? I'm sure Jennifer won't mind if I start my job a bit later."

"Err."

"Becca. We bumped into each other nowhere near where either of us live. This could be the Indian all over again. Let's give fate a chance, hey, and just check in with each other. We missed you." He said.

I couldn't deny that I was happy to see him. My body betrayed me with its faster beating heart and the butterflies in my stomach.

"Okay." I agreed. "I have time for lunch."

"I'll just be a minute." Callum said, heading inside the building I'd just left.

So he'd been seeing a counsellor too. I mulled over our chance meeting as I waited. Callum looked good. His skin was a little paler due to it being the winter. It made his hair seem darker and his eyes stand out more. The scruff on his chin framed his face. He seemed relaxed. Much happier and more confident in his own skin. Or maybe I was projecting. Who knew?

He came back out of the building, a huge smile on his face that made his eyes sparkle. "Okay, I have an hour, let's go find somewhere to eat." There were a few food places on the nearby streets, so we started walking in the direction of the food smells until we decided on a Subway. He insisted on buying both our meals and then we walked upstairs and found a table. While we'd been walking, I'd been telling him about my new house. It seemed something easy and comfortable to chat about.

"We have a lot to catch up on. I'm not sure an hour will be enough." He joked.

I chewed on my bottom lip.

"Out with it, whatever is on the tip of your tongue." He said.

"Well, actually, I do need a few extra sockets putting in at my new property. But I was going to ask someone local."

"No, I'll do it."

"Cal..."

"Becca." He said firmly. "I want to come and nosy at your new home and catch up."

"Can I ask you something?" I said.

"Sure, anything."

"Will you not tell Violet you've seen me? Not at the moment. It's not her; it's just... I'm not sure I want any connections with Willowfield reopened."

He sat straighter and his jaw tightened.

"I'm a connection to Willowfield."

"Yes, but you're here, not there. It's... different."

His eyes met mine and now it was like he wanted to say something. But he didn't.

"I'll come price up the job, and I'll do it on a weekend and say I'm meeting someone. I'll find an excuse."

"Thank you. So, anyway, how have you been?" I asked him. "Did you ever speak to your ex?"

He shook his head. "No. Because there was no result to come from it that would benefit anyone. I didn't want Tali back, and she's getting ready to move on her with her life. I was shown techniques to help me deal with my bitterness about what happened. I'm good. I've been dating again. Nothing serious, but I've been getting back out there. How about you?"

I told him about how I'd given up Rob's part of the house proceeds and bought the house that I'd fallen in love with. How I'd met the single dad for coffee but as a friends thing. Our conversation was comfortable. It wasn't like I hadn't seen him for six months. It was like I'd seen him yesterday and I'd known him forever, and honestly, I didn't know what to do with this feeling. At the same time we were chatting, I was trying to work out what was going on here. But the truth was I just didn't know.

Take it for what it is. A catch up with someone you once knew a little. Someone who cared that you were okay and is still checking in with you.

But I knew deep down that there was more going on here than that. I just didn't know if I was prepared to face up to it.

So instead I carried on chatting until the hour was up and then I gave Callum my new phone number and my new address and arranged for him to call in later after he'd finished his job to price up mine.

We walked back to the counselling offices where I'd left my car. "Right then, I'll see you later." I told him. "You'll see a huge change in Laurel. She's growing up fast."

He nodded. "I bet. Even Milo's grown up in the last six months."

I chuckled at that. "So do you like chicken nuggets, chips, and beans because that's what's on the agenda for tea at a certain girl's request."

"Sounds good to me." He paused. "I'm glad I bumped into you today, Becca. Really glad." He looked nervous.

I took a deep breath. "Yeah, me too."

Cal's body visibly relaxed. "I'll see you tonight."

"Yeah." It was like I didn't want to walk away from him. Just in case something happened and I didn't see him again. The thought struck me to walk back into the counsellors and ask for an emergency appointment because I was clearly losing my mind.

Callum seemed to be the same, not turning for the door.

With a firm resolve, I turned and walked away, got back in my car and drove out of the car park. As I looked in my rear-view mirror, he was still there, watching me leave.

CHAPTER NINETEEN

Callum

When I'd seen Becca I'd thought I was imagining things. You know how you can imagine water in the desert? Well, for a moment I'd thought that maybe I'd dreamed Becca up as she stood in front of me. She'd looked good. Her hair was a little longer, her figure a little fuller. She looked healthy. It was nice to see her not wearing the mask of shame and grief that I'd got used to seeing over those last days before she'd left.

Now I stood on the doorstep of her new house, having just rung the bell. I actually felt a little nervous, like date nervous.

This is not a date, Callum. You're pricing up a

job, remember? I told myself. But I knew I'd not charge Becca anything beyond the materials, and probably not even that.

The door opened and Becca stood there, looking a little less relaxed, a beaming little girl at her side. "Come in. I'm about to burn chicken nuggets and Laurel was mid-tantrum."

She rushed back through to the kitchen while Laurel shouted after her, "I was not, Mummy. I just needed my hair brushed right now."

I closed the door behind me, removed my shoes, hung up my coat and followed the direction they'd gone in.

Laurel stood there with a brush in her hand, waving it at her mum.

"Laurel, baby, I can't do your hair right now. I'm fixing our dinner."

Laurel sighed. "I don't look pretteeeee." She wailed.

I stepped forward. "Miss Laurel, you are the prettiest girl I ever did see."

She looked me over. "My hair is knotty. Grandma said keep it pretty for boys."

Becca whirled around and rolled her eyes at me.

"People should like you for what's inside." I told Laurel.

"Like my tummy?" She said frowning and pressing it with her free hand.

"More like your heart." I replied. "You know; how kind you are."

"I'm kind. Let a spider live in Mummy's bedroom."

Becca looked horrified. I gathered she wasn't keen on eight-legged beasts.

"Do you want to sit at the table, you two, and I'll get us some drinks before I plate up? It's almost ready now."

I took the cutlery from her and began to put it at the side of the placemats.

"We usually only have two people here. You make three. I can count all the way up to twenty." Laurel proceeded to count, missing out the numbers nine and thirteen.

"That's brilliant, Laurel. You're so very clever."

She beamed.

As we ate, it became apparent that we weren't going to get caught up on very much due to a little chatterbox who could barely eat her food around everything she felt she needed to tell me: from who her new friends were, to her new favourite toys.

"Laurel, you need to talk less and eat more." Becca chastised her.

"But, Mummy, Cal came for tea and you said we hadn't seen him for a long time since the old house. He might not come again for a long time."

"I'm coming back on Saturday to put you some new plug sockets in." I told her.

"Oh, okay." She said and started to eat.

I couldn't help but have a chuckle.

Once we'd eaten, I walked around the house and made a note of where Becca told me she wanted her extra sockets. It was a nice house, and I wondered if she missed her old house at all.

"It's a really nice house." I told her.

"As soon as I saw it up for sale, I knew I had to put an offer in. I'd admired it many a time walking to school. Plus, it's near my parents which is a bonus."

"So I gather you're a lot closer to your parents in the emotional sense too now?"

"They've been my rocks and I don't know what I would have done without them, but I'm still someone who likes her own space and privacy and I'm very pleased we now have a place of our own." Her eyes swept around the room and a smile rested on her lips.

"Yeah, I'm wondering about doing the same myself." I confessed.

"What? You're thinking of moving out? Where would you go?" Becca looked genuinely interested, rather than just paying me lip service.

I shrugged. "I've not thought about it, beyond it being a possibility. I just think, I'm twenty-five now and I wouldn't mind a bit more independence. My dad spoke to us all a while back about taking our own parts of the business and becoming our own bosses and I think that's the way for me to go, to become self-employed." I'm thinking out loud and making my mind up to speak to my father about it as I do so.

"Well I'm back working at a supermarket Monday to Wednesday. I'd say it's great because I get a discount on my shopping bill, but I buy far too many packets of biscuits." She patted her stomach.

Though I wanted to compliment her on her figure, I decided not to. It might make her feel awkward. We were only just getting used to each other's company again. "I eat tons of biscuits. They're always being offered along with a cuppa when I'm working."

"Oooh, you can help me eat through my stash

this weekend."

Her statement about me coming back that weekend brought my visit to a timely close. Becca needed to get Laurel's nightly routine underway, and I was ready to get home and veg out on the sofa, hopefully with a can of beer. I might even have a word with Dad.

Saying goodbye to both of them, and confirming I'd see them on Saturday, I drove home. I felt ridiculously happy for someone who'd mainly listened to a three-year-old while eating chicken nuggets. But I'd enjoyed my time with them. *Steady on, Cal.* I had to remind myself that once I'd done the electrics at the weekend that was it; there'd be no reason for me to see Becca again.

I needed to talk to Jules, and ask her advice, because I didn't want it to be the last time. I didn't want that at all.

As I stepped through the doorway of our family home, I thought about how much I'd miss this if I did move out. The blaring lights, the homely smells of food and the hum of the television, along with chattering voices. But maybe Milo moving out was the first sign of the change that needed to come?

Heading into the kitchen to see if anyone had put any beer in the fridge, I found my dad at the sink washing up.

He turned and nodded at me. "You okay, son?"

"Yes thanks, Dad. Been a busy day. Just going to see if there's any beer."

"I bought some on my way home, but I'd grab one quickly; you know how long things like that last in this house."

I took out a can and ripped the top off. It made that satisfying fizzing noise, but thankfully didn't spill out. I swallowed a mouthful and then swiped the back of my hand over my lip. "Dad, do you have time to talk to me about what you said about our businesses and us potentially heading up our own bit?"

"Sure. Let me finish these few dishes and then we could head into the dining room? You go through and I'll see you in there."

"Great. I'll just be getting changed. Meet you in there in ten."

Dad walked in, rubbing at his eyes, and it struck me how tired he looked. "You alright? Not sleeping well?"

He wrinkled up his nose. "I'm okay. This house is just a busy one that's all, especially with young Eli being around more and more. Then I went out last night. I'm not as young as I used to be."

"Oh, you go anywhere nice?"

"Just out for a bite to eat."

I tilted my head and studied my father's face.

"Dad. Did you go out on a date?"

He waved his hand in a 'don't be daft' gesture. "Nah, it was just a bite to eat. A bit of company."

"Anyone I know?"

"Let's chat about this business stuff, shall we? If I ever have anything I want to share about my personal life, I'll let you know."

In other words, 'mind your own business'. I didn't mind that Dad didn't want to talk about it. If he had gone out with someone, then this was new territory for him too as far as I was aware. But I hoped it led onto good things for him; he deserved it.

"So, I've been having a good think about things for a few months now, Dad, and I've decided that I'd very much like to start my own electrical business. You know, take my part of it and run it myself. I know you'd spoken about this, so..."

"I think it's a good idea if you're ready." Dad

said encouragingly. "Just a matter of I don't pay you a salary any more. You work out how you want to run things, and Violet can help you with the secretarial side of things still, until you get on your feet. Then you might want to take on someone yourself. It all depends on how you want to do this. Stay under the umbrella of Waite Home Renovations or fully start out on your own."

"I know I've a lot to think about, including how to balance Waite work alongside any new business."

"If we have jobs that require an electrician, we'll just check your availability and if you're not free we'll set up a database with other trustworthy sparkies. Why not go and be independent, son? It's time you all spread your wings."

"Who'd have thought when Violet moved in last year that she'd set us all off in new directions?" I mused.

"I'm sure we'd have got there eventually, but yeah, when Milo got his girl it was certainly a wake-up call to me that you're all grown ups and should be moving on with your lives. So this is encouraging, Callum. I know you'll be a success. Before you know it, you'll be hiring and moving away from being based at the yard I'm sure."

I decided to get braver.

"I'm thinking I might move out at some point too."

"Hoo-fucking-ray." My father did a little jig. "That'll be three down, three to go."

After saying goodnight to my dad, I walked up to my room while my mind whirled with ideas and possibilities. New house. New business. New opportunities.

As I climbed under my covers, I felt a deep sense of satisfaction and a flutter in my stomach of excitement.

When I dreamt, it was of a new house, with a large garden. I walked into the garden and Laurel was playing there, digging in a sandpit, being helped by Becca. As she saw me, Becca stood up and turned, and I saw her stomach was blossoming. She was having our baby. I walked up and kissed her cheek, stroking my hand down her bump and Laurel looked up beaming with happiness. I heard her say, "Daddy, I built you a sandcastle."

I woke, utterly content until I realised sleep was a cruel hostage taker, and then tears streamed down my cheeks, because no matter what new opportunities came my way, someone having my baby would never be part of it.

CHAPTER TWENTY

Callum

Heading down for breakfast, I found Jules staring into a bowl of cornflakes. "Everything okay, Sis?"

She looked up and yawned. "Yep, just feel like I need a hundred coffees today. You?"

"Everyone else gone?" I asked.

"Yeeaaaasss." She looked me over. "Hmmm, brother wants to talk. Doesn't seem anxious, that's a good sign. Upset, no. But not happy either. Okay, I can't get a read on what the fuck's up with you, so get me another coffee, get what you're having, and let's talk."

And this was why I enjoyed talking things through with my sister. Because she didn't fuck around. If she thought you were being an idiot, you got told straight.

I made us both a drink and I sat near her.

"Do you remember months ago when you thought I might like Becca and I said I didn't know whether it was pity or whether I did like her?"

Jules sat up straighter, looking instantly more awake. "Oooh, colour me intrigued. Yes, I remember. Carry on. The tale of the mysterious widow."

"Honestly, you need to get out more."

"No, actually, I need to get out less, because everywhere I go, that toolbag seems to follow me."

I raised a brow. "And by toolbag you mean Quinn?"

She blew over the top of her drink. "Quinn. Toolbag. Dickhead. They're interchangeable."

Quinn lived at the other side of Milo and Violet. He was a gardener and he seemed to have a keen eye for a pretty flower, like my sister. He kept asking her out. She kept saying no.

"The house I'm working on now. Quinn's doing the garden. He seems to find a lot of excuses to come into the house."

"Just go out with the man once. Show him what a nightmare you are, and he'll be put off forever."

"Hmm."

"You're actually considering it?"

"Maybe, one day, if this carries on. Anyway, back to you. Talk to me. What's happening?"

"I bumped into Becca yesterday, outside the counselling offices of all places and I asked her to get a sandwich with me. I wanted to know what had been happening. Why she'd disappeared without keeping in touch."

"And?"

"And she said she'd just felt it was for the best. That she realised she missed you guys a lot, but that Willowfield held such bad memories, she'd thought it best to just forget the place existed."

"Yeah, nice of her to forget all the people who helped when it counted."

I stared at her.

"I know. I know. She had bigger issues than keeping in touch with Jules Waite. Still, I liked Becca and I missed her. You know, I don't have many female friends, or friends at all for that matter."

"Well she seemed a lot more settled. She'd just

moved into a place with her and Laurel and she'd even been out for a coffee with a single dad."

I felt my body posture tighten as I said it.

"And you didn't like hearing that because you like her?"

I nodded my head. "I do, but I can't pursue it, can I? What if it's still too early or what if she doesn't like me back?"

Jules took a sip of her drink while she mulled things over.

"Well, how did you leave it after the lunch? Did you just say goodbye? Because if you did, I think that's a solid signal that she still doesn't want anything to do with us."

"She invited me for tea and asked me to price up fitting extra sockets in her house."

Jules smirked. "Oh, I think she likes you, Cal boy."

I took a deep breath. "You think?"

"Not only did she invite you for tea, she asked you to price up a job meaning that you'd have to go back again. There are plenty of electricians where she lives, Cal. And even then, if she just wanted your electrical expertise, she didn't need to provide a meal."

"I don't know what to do. What do I do?"

"You realise who you're asking for dating advice, right? The person who hasn't had a proper boyfriend, ever."

"I still want your advice."

"Okay, so if I did ever date, these are my thoughts. Go and do the job she wants you to do. When is that?"

"Tomorrow."

"Okay. Go do that and just chat and see how you get on. Try to listen to what she's saying. Is she asking about you specifically when she talks, and showing more than a polite interest, or is she just making polite conversation. Or is it Violet and me she misses and that's who she asks about."

"Fuck, this is complicated. I feel like there should be an exam to pass first."

"Love is complicated, which is why I try to avoid it. Anything for a simple life, that's me. Anyway, don't mention anything else until the job's done because you don't want anything awkward to happen where you end up wanting to leave and the work isn't finished. You need to wait until it's almost time to go home and then see if she makes an excuse to try to get you back *again*. If she does, she is very interested. Okay?"

"Okay."

"Or of course she might just have thought of something else she needs doing. Can't be one hundred per cent."

I placed my forehead in my hand. "I think you've helped. Hard to be sure."

"You're welcome."

"So what are you plastering at the moment. Sounds a busy house if Quinn is there too."

"It's a decent sized house. The couple are having it modernised before they move in."

"I'm thinking of getting my own place."

"Seriously? Wow."

"I could do what that couple are doing. Buy somewhere that needs a little work and renovate it before I move into it. Call on all my siblings to help."

"Yeah, there's nothing we'd like better than to spend our spare time doing what we do in our working hours." Jules said sarcastically.

"Shit, I didn't think of it that way." I finished my drink.

"I'm joking, Cal. Of course we'd all come and help you. That's what family does, and if we can't help each other when we're all so supremely talented, then it'd be a waste. I'm in to plaster any walls. It's not like I have a life anyway."

"Go out with Quinn."

"Focus on your own love life." Jules seemed to be thinking of something. She opened her mouth, but then didn't say anything.

"You got something to add?" I asked.

"It's good to see that you're thinking of the future. I know I've already said it but I'm proud of you for going to see someone. Really proud. Do you finally think you've gained the closure you needed about Tali?"

I stood and got myself another cup of tea, before sitting back down.

"I can live with it as it is." I answered truthfully. "I can't know whether it would have been better to talk to her or not, but the chances are it wouldn't have solved anything as ultimately we aren't each other's future. I loved her. Deeply loved her. But the cracks that had shown before the wedding would have meant we'd have split up eventually if we'd gone through with it. I truly believe that. Like I said to you all before, she wanted her own children." I'd told them everything just after Becca had left. Decided to let the rest of my family in on what had happened in my past.

Jules chewed on her bottom lip. "So if I said she

would like to talk to you, would you want to go to see her?"

I put my cup down on the table so hard, tea splashed over the edges.

"What's going on, Jules?"

She looked up at me. "The house I'm plastering. It's Tali and her fiance's. I know for a fact that the reason she employed me was as a route to get to you. Her fiancé knows I'm your sister and he doesn't care. He's called Hugh. He's nice."

Jules was working on Tali's house? I couldn't get my head around it. "Where's the house?"

"Danesford. On the next street to her parents' house."

"Figures."

"She knows that something doesn't add up, Cal. She said to me that the Cal she knew wouldn't have left her at the altar. That he loved her too much to do that. She said now her anger has gone and she's found love again, she feels that more than ever there was more to it and she wants to talk to you. She asked me if you would be willing to go and speak to her."

I just sat there, no doubt looking like I didn't know what I should do with this information.

"When she asked, I said I doubted you'd want

to, but after this conversation, I think you'd both benefit from it. I think you should talk to her, Cal. I really do. Finish this thing once and for all."

"It's not as simple as that though, is it? If I tell her about her father, he might send his people after you again."

"Her father had a stroke a few months ago. He's in a care home and unlikely to regain his power of speech."

My jaw dropped.

"You get to tell your story with no comeback, Cal. To me it's a no brainer. Go get closure."

Could I do this? Could I go see my past and tell her the truth? Maybe we owed it to each other to clear the past away. She could go and happily marry her new fiancé, and I could... what?

Be a free man, Cal. Truly.

"Give me her number. I'll arrange to see her next week." I said.

Jules took out her mobile phone and read me the digits off and I put them into my own phone. Fuck, there it was just like old times. The name Tali and her number.

Only now she was no longer mine, but someone else's.

And I felt totally okay with that, as I was no longer hers.

I was beginning to see that my heart had maybe never wholly belonged to her at all. It seemed a little tiny corner of it had stayed in an Indian restaurant years ago.

CHAPTER TWENTY-ONE

Becca

All the way through Callum being at my house yesterday, the same question had been running through my mind. Was Callum just a friend, or did I see him in another way entirely?

After he'd left, and I'd got Laurel settled and in bed, I'd sat on my sofa with a glass of wine and replayed the evening in my head. I'd already spent the time before he came for dinner replaying every piece of conversation from our lunch over and over, and now I had another couple of hours of conversation to try to decipher too. I'd never been very good at this dating lark to start with. It was why my friend had set me up on the blind date with Rob in the first place. She'd felt I'd needed a helping hand.

My whole thought processes were pointless. I had absolutely no clue whether Callum liked me in anything other than a friend way. Plus, was I really ready to embark on dating and a potential relationship anyway? I just got Laurel and I set up in our new home and maybe right now that was enough. But conversely—and this was why I was giving myself a headache—everything with Rob still made me feel that life was short and if you'd got an opportunity for happiness you should seize it with both hands. In other words, I didn't have a fucking clue what to do.

It was times like these that I missed having Violet in my life and regretted my decision to cut off contact with her. Don't get me wrong, I had made some new friends amongst the mothers at nursery and occasionally I met them for coffee. But conversation always revolved around the kids. No one had the guts to raise a conversation with a widow and ask her if she was thinking of dating again. Oh I was sure they wanted to know the answer, but it appeared the residents of Hill Green were extremely polite. Even Todd, the single dad who I'd had a coffee with, had made it clear that he was asking me as a friend and respected the fact I was a widow. I wondered what he would have said if I'd have demanded he fucked me over the café's table?

I wasn't someone who dithered. I was someone who sledgehammered my way through to getting what I wanted and needed. It had been six months. Six goddam months! Even frikking longer if you thought about the fact that my husband hadn't been sexually interested in me at all in the months before he died, given that I was obviously too freaking old for him. Yes, I could even have a little laugh with myself now about the past. God only knows I'd needed it.

So I was going to spend Saturday seeing how Callum and I got along and somehow I would test out the waters to see whether he might want to take me out some time. *Fuck it*, I thought to myself. If not, he lived a thirty minute drive away from Hill Green. I'd probably never have to see him again.

And yet the next morning, while Laurel sat on the landing playing with her favourite toys, the stairgate safely closing her off from danger, I was in the bathroom defuzzing bits that had not been defuzzed for a long, long time, and telling myself that it had absolutely nothing to do with a certain

Waite brother coming around the next day. But the truth was, the electrician coming tomorrow was sparking feelings in me I could no longer deny.

By the time Saturday came around, I was beside myself with nervous energy. I'd hardly slept, and when Laurel had woken me at six am, instead of cursing the early start, I'd leapt out of bed, got her up and breakfasted and then went and put on the outfit I'd selected to wear: a pair of skinny jeans that I hoped showed my legs and butt to their best advantage and a soft cream Cashmere jumper that came to my waist, therefore not covering my butt and hopefully clinging nicely over my boobs. Then I put on some light make-up that I hoped highlighted my best features: my eyes and lips.

When the doorbell eventually went at nine am, it was a race to the door as Laurel had spotted Cal walking up the driveway from the window where she'd been playing with her dolls.

"Cal, you came back!" She said, smiling away.

I wished him a good morning and asked him to come in, but my daughter wouldn't leave his side and so any other conversation between us was lost for a time as she chattered away about everything and anything.

"I'm sorry, she can really talk." I said to Cal as I passed him a drink of tea.

"Yeah, I'm noticing." He laughed. "Don't worry about it. I'll be busy soon and then she'll get bored."

"Don't bet on it."

"You two going out anyway?"

"Sorry?"

He nodded at my clothing. "You look dressed up. I thought you must be going somewhere."

"Oh, no. I just—"

Cal's face paled. "Oh God, sorry, Becca. I forgot you always look clean, tidy, and presentable. I'm used to my own family. We permanently look like a group of vagrants."

Clean, tidy, and presentable. I felt like he'd kicked me in the gut.

Clean.

Tidy.

And fucking presentable.

What? Like I was going to a job interview? Like I looked like a bloody librarian?

For a moment I wished I had a black PVC catsuit in my wardrobe and then I'd bloody show him about clean, tidy, and presentable.

"You okay, Becca?"

"Huh?"

"You're staring into space."

"Oh, sorry, was miles away then. Right, I'd better leave you to it. We'll try to keep out of your way. You remembered to not bring any lunch? I've made us something. Laurel got all excited about the idea of an indoor picnic."

"Sounds fab. Now not to be cheeky, but have you got any of those biscuits you spoke about on Thursday?" Cal winked.

I wished that wink had been received in response to my efforts to look nice.

Fuck my life.

And then Laurel decided she didn't like the noise the drill made in the wall and so we had to camp upstairs in my bedroom, so I didn't get to say another word to him. He ended up having to make his own drinks after the first time I tried to leave Laurel and she clung to my leg screaming.

Finally, lunchtime came around and Cal downed tools and came and sat in the kitchen at our table.

"Noooooo." Laurel wouldn't let me pick her up, her arms going around her waist. "Picnic."

"Yes, we're having the picnic, Laurel. You need to sit at the table so we can eat."

"Noooooo."

Exasperated, I looked over to Cal. "I'm sorry, I don't know what's wrong with her today."

"I think I do." Cal said. "Give me a couple of minutes."

He went into the living room and I heard the front door open. A few minutes later he was back.

"Okay, come through. Is this what you want, Laurel?"

Laurel ran off into the room and I heard her shout, "Picnic," before I saw her sit down on a blanket I'd never seen before.

"I keep it in the back of the van. Do you need any help carrying things through? I guessed Laurel wanted a proper picnic, where you sit on a blanket."

"God, I feel stupid for not figuring that out myself. Everything is in a basket if you'd carry that in and then I'll just bring the orange juice. I'll make us a hot drink to go with dessert as that's still in the fridge."

"Wow, I am being spoiled." Callum smiled.

"It's the least I can do. Anyway, we have to eat."

Why did I say that? Now it looked like I didn't

make an effort for him, that we'd have been doing this anyway. This was just all going wrong. It had not been the morning I'd imagined at all.

Luckily, lunch went a lot better. All I'd needed was to put Laurel's favourite foods out. She was too busy stuffing her face with cocktail sausages to pay us any attention. I'd got out her pretend tea set and she was pretending to feed her favourite toys Luna and Hugo in between.

"So tell me more about Eli. I presume he's much more part of things now you've known him for six months."

"Yep. It's like a divorce arrangement now. He stays every other weekend. And we still go bowling every Saturday night whether he's staying or not. Can't remember him not being part of things. And despite him saying he was academic, he loved watching me do my work and now says he wants to study to be an electrician, so it looks like in a couple of years I might have an apprentice."

"Oh wow. And what does Angela think to that?"

"She's fine with it all. Just happy to see him happy. Now she knows we're not taking him away from her, I think she looks forward to him being at ours. Gives her some time off the teenage years!"

"Oh don't. I keep being warned about those. Laurel has her moments now. I'm dreading adding hormones to the mix."

"You're a great mum. You'll be fine. Plus, you never know, you might have met someone by then."

Okay, he was looking at me. Was that in an 'I mean me' way or was he just generally telling me I might meet someone else? What could I ask him back? Think, Becca, think.

"You never know. I'm certainly not averse to the idea now."

Ask me out. Ask me out.

"What about coffee dad? He sounded interested?"

And there we had it. He was suggesting I dated coffee dad. My innards flinched with disappointment.

"Hmmm, maybe. I didn't get any vibes from him other than friend ones though. He wasn't really my type. How about you?"

"The dates I've been on haven't been anything special. I took Lisa out; you know, the barmaid from the Half Moon."

"Yeah, you said before." *And I don't like thinking about it any more now than I did last time around.*

"Oh yes, when we talked about being friend-zoned. Well, I've dated a few women since then but none of it's been anything serious."

If my stomach twisted up any further, I'd need a hospital.

"Funny story, Lisa now lives in your old house."

"What?"

"Yeah. She's renting it."

"Oh."

"She's become good friends with Vi and Jules."

Phone 999, it's an emergency. I have a massive hernia because someone pinched my friends. I cruelly abandoned them and now karma is kicking my arse hard. I'm being replaced.

"That's nice."

"Your face."

I snapped my head up, my eyes firmly on his.

"What do you mean?"

"You're jealous. It's written all over your face. Completely and utter jealous."

Hallelujah. He'd realised. Thank God. Now kiss me already, dumbarse.

"You miss them, don't you?"

"Who?"

What was he talking about now? Why was he not kissing me?

"Violet and Jules. You lost touch with them and now you're totally jealous they're friends with Lisa. It's not too late to pick up the phone you know?"

I hoped he thought the bone-crushing disappointment now showing across my features was due to 'how much I missed my old friends'. Gah.

"I know. Maybe one day. So there's no one special in your life then?" *Back to you and dating, Cal. Back. To. You.*

Don't let me down.

He took a deep breath. "I'm going to see Tali next week." He said.

Of all the things I anticipated him saying, that was not one of them. I gave up any hope of him having any interest in me. The expression on his face was one of hope.

"Oh, gosh. Shit, look at the time. I'd better let you get back to work." I told him.

And then I began to clear things away and left him alone. It was rude, but I didn't want to hear about him meeting up with his ex. Not one single word.

CHAPTER TWENTY-TWO

Callum

Well today couldn't have been any more awkward if Rob had returned from the dead and walked into the house.

We'd not been able to talk much because Laurel had decided she was scared shitless of my drill and then lunch had been a disaster.

I didn't get any vibes that Becca was particularly ready to start dating. In fact, she'd shown more emotion about Lisa taking over her old life than interest in romance. I got it though. When something so huge had happened in your past, it took a lot of confidence to start again.

I couldn't believe that when I'd mentioned

Tali, Becca had ended lunch and walked away. She was the one who'd encouraged me to get that closure and now she didn't seem interested. And then I understood. She'd taken herself away from Willowfield. Had cut all ties. She probably realised now that getting me to come here was a mistake and wanted me to do the job and go home. Back to my own world and leaving her to hers.

My chest filled with a crushing disappointment, but at least now I knew. My feelings were one-sided. She didn't want any part of her old life back; she'd moved on.

I carried on adding the sockets where she'd wanted them while she kept Laurel occupied away from the main noise. I made my own drinks, and after I'd finished, I washed my mug and cleared up the brick dust.

"Becca." I shouted up the stairs. But all I could hear was Laurel screeching with excitement about something.

Was there actually any point in me saying goodbye? I picked up my tools and walked outside, closing the door firmly behind me. Once in the van, I sent a text.

All done. I tried to shout you, but you didn't hear. You just need someone to

plaster where I've had to drill into the walls and then a spot of painting and you're done. Take care. Cal.

And then I drove away.

By the time I got home I'd received a text back.

Becca:Thank you. Sorry, I didn't get to say goodbye. You did an amazing job. I need to pay you for it.

Cal:No payment necessary. I was doing a favour for an old friend.

Becca:Well, thank you. Thank you for having been such a good friend. PS less of the old.

But I wasn't focusing on her joke. I was staring at the world 'been'. Past tense.

It was time to draw a line under Becca and move on. Part of which was going to speak to my ex.

. . .

Jules came to sit with me that night and asked how I'd got on. She was the only family member who knew where I'd been; I'd not even confided in Milo.

"She made it clear she was done with all of us, Jules. Although on saying that, when I said you and Vi were friends with Lisa, she'd looked really pissed off."

"I'm not being funny, but you're a guy. You can't even find the butter if I put it on a different shelf. Are you sure she wasn't interested? Maybe you were just too chicken shit to find out."

"I said I was going to see Tali and she dismissed me. Didn't want to hear about me hopefully gaining some closure in my life. It was crystal clear."

Jules sighed.

"I know, it's crap. But I just have to deal with it. At least she got some extra sockets out of the situation. I'm not sure what I got except frustrated." I stretched and yawned. "Right, I'm off to bed."

Jules nodded, but she was deep in thought, probably wondering when any more of us Waites might actually get lucky in love.

At eleven am on Monday, I pulled up outside the newly painted front door of my ex's new home. It was good that as an electrician I could move work around to fit in with my increasingly disrupted life-style. I was going to have to get better organised and have less drama in my life when I started this as my own business.

The thought of CW Electrical Services was becoming more exciting every day. I'd started making lists of what I needed such as a logo, and I kept dreaming of the future when I had a team and it included Eli. I knew that this might not actually happen and the kid had time to decide to do many other things with his life, but I liked dreaming about the possibilities.

In fact, I reckoned in a week's time, Eli might just decide he wanted to be an actor, because Ezra was coming over. He had a premiere in London a week on Friday which nicely coincided with half-term, so he was taking Eli and Angela with him and had roped me in to come along, because he'd be having to 'schmooze' as he put it.

Yes, I'd daydreamed that I'd meet one of his attractive co-stars on the red carpet and she'd whisk me backstage for some hot action. It helped to take my mind off a certain other female.

I climbed out of my van and rang the doorbell and then there she was.

Tali.

Looking nervous as hell while trying to pretend she wasn't. She'd forgotten I knew every move of her body.

"Hey, Tali. I still take my tea the same way if you're making some."

She relaxed a little at that and smiled. "Come in."

I stepped over the threshold and went to remove my shoes.

"Oh no, don't do that. The house is messy. You'll need to keep them on."

"Oh, okay." I followed her down the hall into a vast kitchen and dining space that looked over a huge back garden with decking and a large lawn. It had been a long time since I'd visited Danesford and saw how the other half lived.

"Jules told me about your father, Tali. I'm sorry."

"Are you?" She said. "Because if he'd done to me what he'd done to you, I wouldn't be sorry at all."

I stood stock still.

"Did Jules—"

She shook her head. "No. My mother told me. She's been telling me a lot of things since he became unable to control her. I can't believe what he did to you, and... and that he let me stand at a church and get jilted, all to destroy our relationship." She went to pick up two mugs. "Let me make these drinks and then we can go through to the living room. That's finished, so you'll have to leave your shoes outside of that room, but we can talk. Properly talk."

"Okay."

I stayed silent while she made the drinks and then I followed her into the living room.

Walking into the brightly lit space that had sliding patio doors at one side that took up the whole wall, I was struck by the clean looking lines, and I knew that although my own place would be nothing as grand as this, I liked the lack of clutter and would try to emulate something similar but on a smaller scale. Our house always had things left around with how many of us lived there: books, magazines, papers, clothing, mugs, wrappers, discarded post, and looked cluttered.

"I love this room." I remarked. "Your tastes have changed then? This looks nothing like how you decorated our place."

Tali laughed and it was nice to see her relaxing in my company. "Yeah, sorry about my vintage phase and all the antiques."

I shrugged my shoulders. "I liked it at the time, but now I'm more into this. Clean lines and space. I'm thinking of getting my own place."

There were two cream sofas in the living room and she sat on one while I took the other. She was dressed in wide legged yoga pants and a long slouchy top, both in pale pink, and her blonde hair was up in a high ponytail. She looked healthy and happy. I'd dressed in my beige chinos, thank fuck, because I didn't want the dye from my jeans transferring to these sofas. I'd probably need a mortgage for the repairs.

"I can't believe that almost all of you are still living at home. Well, actually I can, because you were always so close. I envied you having so many siblings when I had none. Hugh has three sisters and a brother, so I finally feel like I have some family."

"I'm glad you met someone, Tali. Congratulations. I hope you're not freaking out about turning up to church."

She smiled but it was tinted with sadness. "No, I know Hugh will be there. My father did approve of him." She turned to me. "I know you'd have been there too if it wasn't for him. Things could have been very different, couldn't they?"

And this was where the real conversation was about to start. All the things we'd never got to say before.

"I wouldn't have been there, Tali. But neither would you. We'd have cancelled the wedding."

She pursed her lips in thought and I could guess what she was thinking. Wondering how I'd come to that conclusion given the wedding was still going ahead as far as she knew.

"I heard you talking to your friend just before the wedding. Telling her how you didn't know if you wanted to go through with it."

She shook her head. "I was just panicking."

I smiled, my eyes hopefully conveying my thoughts that it was okay. "Tali. If we'd have gone through with the wedding, eventually we'd have split up. I heard the truth in your voice that night. You were being honest with your friend; an honesty you'd not shown me. I get it now. You loved me and you had pretty fucking difficult choices to make. The man you love versus the children you didn't have yet."

"I would have been there. I would have chosen you." She said softly.

I nodded. "I know you would, and then we'd have embarked on starting our fostering or adoption process and you'd have spent the time wondering if you did the right thing. Then as problems arose and it got tricky—because adoption is a rocky road—you'd have begun to resent me. Your father would have been loading additional pressure onto you for not giving him a biological grandchild. Plus, your biological clock would never have stopped ticking because you can have them. It's me who can't."

A tear slipped down her cheek. "I'm sorry."

She wasn't apologising for me not being able to have children. We'd been through all that years ago. She was apologising because she knew I spoke the truth. It wasn't the life she'd wanted to live.

"You'd have tried, because you loved me; and I would have let you go because I loved you."

Walking over to her, we went into each other's arms and in that embrace let out all our 'sorry's' and I was so pleased that she had reached out through Jules, because finally here was real closure for us both. It was a shame that as she was in my arms, once again my mind went to another female who I'd held within them. Another closed door.

Once we'd composed ourselves and Tali returned from the downstairs bathroom after excusing herself to wash her face, she fixed us both a sandwich and then took me on a tour of the house. Jules was in the master bedroom plastering.

She smiled but kept her gaze on me, silently asking if I was okay. "Good work, Jules." I told her, and she nodded her head, catching my subtle undertones that everything was working out just fine.

"I love your house, Tali. It's making me even more excited about getting my own. I think when I get home tonight, I'm going to check out Rightmove and seriously begin looking around."

"That's great news, Cal. It's time. It really is. You went back home when you needed your family around you, but I don't think you do anymore. Jules said there's not been anyone significant since us, but that you're starting to date again. That's good. That's really good."

"It's very strange us talking about dating and marrying other people isn't it?"

She laughed. "Weird as fuck, but I'm glad we are talking."

"Me too."

"I know it would be completely inappropriate for us to stay in touch, but don't be a stranger, Cal. Keep my number and when you meet someone let me know. I want to know you're happy. It would mean the world to me to know that."

"Okay. But I am happy, Tali. I'm in a good place right now." I realised as I said it, that it was the truth. "I'm about to look for a new house, and to go into business for myself. I'm dating again, and although I don't know what the future holds as to whether or not I'll find my way to fatherhood of any kind, I've got a younger brother who I'm trying to be a good role-model to. Right now, I'm okay."

"He's lucky to have you looking out for him." She squeezed my arm.

"How come you've not had any children yet?" I asked the question Becca had raised with me.

"I got so wrapped up in what was happening with my friends that I became obsessed with the thought of motherhood. But I wanted it for all the wrong reasons. It was hard, but when everything happened I kind of went through a period of loss. All my options to motherhood had gone and along with that was the devastation of what I thought had happened. I moved away, which my father hated, but I needed space. I took a business course and focused on my career instead. Then I met Hugh along the way and slowly found myself again. He helped put me back together, but ultimately, I did it myself. Unwittingly, my father made me more independent than ever."

"Well, it looks good on you."

"Thanks. I hope I get to have kids. It is what I want, and we're going to try after the wedding, but I'm just concentrating on now. That's what we have, now. We don't know what the future will bring, do we?"

Moving closer, I gave Tali another squeeze. "I wish you every happiness, Tali, truly. I'm glad you were part of my life, but I wish you so much love and happiness with Hugh. Good luck with everything."

"Thank you. You too. Go be a huge success, get that house and go get a girl."

Then I left, waving at Tali at the doorway and feeling a peace settle over me that I'd not felt in a long time.

One day, I'd find love again. I knew it. But for now, I had a pretty amazing life and I was determined to live it to the best of my ability. And to start, I was going to look for a new place to live. A renovation project. Tali's house had given me ideas and I wanted something I could get relatively cheap because it was a wreck and do up. I knew from when we'd renovated Violet's house that the Waite family could turn things around at a rapid pace, but if it actually took me a few months, I wouldn't mind at all. Eli could come help. I'd bet he'd love that.

But for now, it was off to my next job, to fix some electrics and bring joy to someone else's life.

CHAPTER TWENTY-THREE

Becca

If I believed in signs from the universe, I'd take it that Callum Waite was not meant to be part of my life after all, despite our fateful meetings along the way. I couldn't believe that my daughter had made so much noise I'd not heard him leave. Well... actually, I could believe that, but I felt so bad, and rude, at letting him come and sort out the sockets, take no payment, and just give him a sandwich and the cold shoulder.

I should have listened to him when he started to talk to me about seeing Tali. All those times he'd been there for me and in his time of need, I'd walked away. I was a bitch. Pure and simple.

In fact, the more I thought about how I'd walked away from Violet and the Waites, I realised that although I'd been protecting myself in some ways and making a fresh start, in others I'd been a complete and utter selfish bitch.

And now I'd succeeded in driving these people out of my life, I wanted them back in it. My mother would argue I'd always been this awkward, I thought, as I pulled up outside her house ready to pick up Laurel. I'd done my shift and Mum and Dad would have picked up Laurel from nursery. On a Monday evening, my mum cooked for us all before we went home.

As I was helping her wash the dishes after we'd eaten, she looked me up and down and spoke.

"Out with it, Becca. I know something's eating at you. I've seen that same face too many times before."

"I messed up, Mama."

I saw the alarm pass over her face and I patted her arm.

"Not in any serious way. Just when I moved here and I lost touch with my friends from Willowfield."

"The woman next door?" She asked.

"Yeah, and Jules across the way. I stopped all

contact and then the other day I bumped into Jules' brother, Callum. He was the one who put me the extra sockets in on Saturday. I realised that I'd been selfish. They were so kind and I cut them off. I walked away."

"Becca, you had just lost your husband, and there was all the drama. No one would blame you for any of how you acted during that time if they were a true friend. Just get in touch if you want them in your life again. You've nothing to lose by sending a text." She held up both hands in a weighing things up way, "except maybe the cost of the text, and some pride."

"You really think I should? I mean it might mean me sometimes going back to Willowfield and facing people."

Mum put a hand on each hip. "You put your head up high in that place. You did nothing wrong. They probably forgot it by now anyway. There'll always be new gossip come to take the old's place."

I knew she was right. I couldn't let thoughts of something that might happen get in the way of me reaching out. And I'm Becca Bolton. I don't take any shit, not from anyone. It's about time I stood up for what I wanted in my life, and I wanted my friends back.

"So let's have the rest of it. This man who has your head in a spin. Callum."

"What? No one has my head in a spin."

She gave me side-eye. "You know every time you told me you'd enjoyed my coconut and sweet potato pudding, and I knew you were full of it and I'd find it halfway down the kitchen bin... this is the same tale you're trying to spin me, sweetie. You got it bad. It's why you're walking around like you're constipated."

"Mama!"

"Don't 'Mama' me. Out with it, because these dishes are almost done and Laurel will have worn your father out by now."

"Okay, I like Callum Waite; but he doesn't like me."

She cocked a hip. "He doesn't like you, but he came all the way over here from Willowfield to fix your sockets and I bet he didn't charge you for his work either."

I looked guilty.

"Wake yourself up, girl. What you waiting for, a diamond?"

I chewed on my bottom lip. "You really think he might like me back?"

"Is the grass green? Get your friends back and go get your man, Becca."

I smiled. "I'll try, Mama. I'll try."

As it turned out, a text I received while driving home took any decisions away from me.

Unknown number: It's Jules. I took your number from Cal's phone. You had those sockets plastered yet because we need to talk?

I sent a text back.

Becca: That's the strangest thing. I was driving home when I got your message and I'd just been talking to my mum about getting back in touch with you and Violet. I'm so sorry for abandoning our friendship.

Jules: You can apologise by buying a nice chocolate cake to go with all the coffee you'll provide me with. What day am I coming?

Becca:I work Monday through Wednesday, so Thursday? I take Laurel to nursery in the afternoon, so I get a

couple of hours where I can talk without a three-year-old interrupting.

Jules: Okay, I'll move some things around. Half one, Thursday?

Becca:Sure.

Jules: We missed you.

Becca: I missed you too.

Jules did indeed turn up at my door just after half past one on the Thursday. She stepped inside and looked around the place.

"Nice place."

"Thanks."

I started to explain about giving Rob's share of the house proceeds away, but she held a hand up. "I know everything, Becca. Over the last couple of days, I've made it my mission to extract every piece of information I can from my brother. And now I know where his head is at, I've come to find out what's happening in yours. Then I may bang them both together."

I just stood staring at her for a moment. "Ohhkaaayy. Well, first I'll make you that coffee and I bought a cake."

Where I usually went for what I wanted, Jules was the kind of girl who called a spade a spade, so it didn't surprise me when after finishing off a slice of cake—priorities, right?—she just came right out with what was on her mind.

"Do you like my brother, Becca? And I'll be clear. I mean Callum, and I mean like as in do you want him to take you on a date and maybe rock your world. No fudging or fumbling around, trying to work out what Callum's own answer was. Yes or no?" She folded her arms across her chest.

I stared at her tattoos because I was too nervous to meet her eyes.

"Yes."

"Thank fuck for that. Becca, Callum feels the same way about you."

"But he hasn't shown any interest and he went to see Tali."

Her brow creased. "To finally get closure. She's marrying someone else. She's happy. They had a good talk and they can now both properly move on. He doesn't have any feelings for his ex." She huffed a breath out. "Now can you see why I threatened to bang your heads together?"

"But he said I could go out with coffee date guy?"

She shook her head. "Can't see him saying that at all."

"He did. He said 'what about coffee dad?' They were his exact words."

Jules looked at me like I'd failed my two-times-table. "And do you think that could have been him subtly testing the waters to see if you were interested in anyone else?"

I put my drink down. "Oh." I paused as the penny truly dropped. "Ohhhhh."

Jules' eyes widened while she waited.

"Does Callum really like me back?"

"Duh."

I squealed. Fully on girly squealed. "Seriously, like wants to date me and might want to rock my world?"

"Double-duh."

I took a bite out of a second slice of cake, and then after I swallowed it, I couldn't help but beam, no doubt showing Jules my chocolate covered teeth.

"Oh my god. I don't know what to do with this information. Do I call him? Will he call me?"

"I'll tell you what's going to happen." Jules informed me. "You're going to ask your parents to babysit Laurel overnight this weekend and then on

Saturday you're going to turn up to family bowling night and no one will know you're coming, except me and Violet." She stared at me again. Her face clearly said that was the plan, end of. "And tonight, you're going to ring Violet and apologise profusely for binning her off as a friend, and do you know how you'll know exactly what to say?" She gave me an evil smirk.

"Because I'm going to do that to you right now?"

"Duh." She repeated.

And that was exactly what I did. I apologised and then Jules told me how she fully understood why I'd distanced myself and we hugged like crazy before she had to leave.

And that night once Laurel was tucked up in bed, I picked up the phone and dialled the number I'd kept in my address book. The one I'd double-checked with Jules before she'd left.

"Becca." Vi said as she answered.

"Hi, stranger. Is this a good time for me to apologise for being MIA?"

"Just give me a moment to grab a glass of water and then yes. Only I've a feeling we might be on this call a while, given you have a lot to catch me up on."

She was right. It was over two hours later that I

finally put the phone down. My throat felt a little sore from talking so much, but it had been amazing to catch up, and I had to admit Lisa sounded like a nice woman and I looked forward to getting to know her too. I'd meet her in two day's time. Though I wasn't sure I'd get much chance to talk to her then.

Violet knew the main reason I was coming bowling and on this occasion it wasn't to see my friends.

I was coming to get my man.

At least I hoped I was.

CHAPTER TWENTY-FOUR

Callum

It was Friday evening and Silas had dragged me out to the pub. After fetching us both a pint he sat across from me and took a few large gulps from his.

"Steady on, bro. You been working up a thirst?" I asked him.

"Sure have." He winked. "Now, spill. Where have you been going every night this week?" He leant closer to me.

"How do you know I've been going anywhere? You're never in."

"Hmmm, not answering the question. Are you seeing someone, Callum Waite?"

I sniggered at him. "Look at you. Never had you pegged as a gossip queen. Hanging around with all those housewives is rubbing off on you."

"Yeah, instead of him rubbing off on them." Came a familiar voice as Milo took a seat at the side of us.

Silas rolled his eyes. "We need another pint each, Miley. Then hurry up. I'm trying to find out where Cal's been going every night this week."

"Oh, I already know that. Anyone else joining us?" He asked.

"Nope. Just us three tonight. Off you go then." Silas ordered him.

"You're gonna be bitterly disappointed." Milo told him, walking away.

"So...?"

"I've been looking at houses." I put him out of his misery.

Surprise hit his features. "You're moving out?"

I nodded. "Eventually. I'm going to get a reno project. That way I can get something larger, more bang for my buck, and make sure it's exactly the way I want it. Make rooms bigger if needed etc. Might as well make the most of having a family of tradesmen."

"Good on you, Cal. Though I'm disappointed you've not been shagging about."

"I've had a few dates lately." I reassured him. "Nothing on your level, but a few. How's the world of fitness been this week?"

"Fabulous, though I've been told by my customers there's a new instructor recently set up. Not going to bother me though cos she's female. Even if she is trying to undercut me with her introductory offers, it's not going to affect the clients who are with me because I put the fit into fitness instructor."

"Always so shy." I snarked.

Milo put the beers down on the table and sat back.

"How come you've deigned to provide us with your company tonight?" I asked him.

"Vi's on the phone, gossiping away with a mate. She threw me out. Said my hanging around was getting on her nerves. I think she's getting bored with me." He affected a sad expression, then he sniggered. "I've told her she's got until closing and then I'm coming back and if she's not off the phone, I'll put something in her mouth that stops her conversation."

"Oh yeah, what did she say to that?" I asked.

"That she'd bite it off." He guffawed. "Fuck, I love that woman."

"Yeah, I think we all know." Silas said. "Now, Cal, tell me more about these houses."

"Okay so one is here in Willowfield, actually on Willowfield Road. It's a three-bedroomed semi-detached. Just in need of modernising, but inside rooms are fine, decent sizes."

"But...?"

"I just feel like stretching myself a little beyond that. So I found a place in Hill Green."

"Isn't that where Becca lives?" Milo helpfully pointed out.

"Yeah. This one's right at the other side of there though. It's a barn, ripe for conversion with a small amount of land. Planning permission has already been granted for a four bedroomed home. I reckon there's a possibility I could get the planning amended so that I could make the far end of the barn an office or get a different planning order for a separate annex. I don't need much for CW Electrical Services."

"Oooh, get you." Milo elbowed me.

"This is amazing. It has to be the Hill Green one, without a doubt. I'll help you for sure. What about you, Miley?"

"He had me at 'barn conversion'. I reckon there'll be plenty for me to smash my way through and build up." He held up an arm. "Gotta keep these guns strong for carrying my missus up to the bedroom."

"Do you want to come and see the place tomorrow? I was going to take a second look at eleven before I put an offer in. I was hoping I'd be able to get a few of you to come."

"Absolutely." They both said. Then, as we sat and enjoyed our beers, inwardly I got ridiculously excited as I knew I wanted that place. It was perfect for my future plans. I just had to hope no one beat me to it.

The following morning, I was at the property with the whole of my family. I couldn't believe that every single one of them had turned up. The estate agent had looked bemused as I introduced her to them all. As we walked around the barn and the land, all my brothers and Jules noted the things they could do and help with. My dad stayed by my side and we walked around the land together.

"I'd separate the office from the barn, Cal." He began pointing at the area. "While you're in business, you can use all the space, but if you put your office over there." He pointed to the other side of the plot. "Then come retirement, or if you needed to, you could sell that half of the land."

"Good thinking. I've only been considering the next few years, but I could easily split this space if needed. I'd still have the barn and some decent land for a garden. The plans for the barn incorporate a double garage, and there's ample driveway from the side road. I can put the office where you suggest and run a separate driveway to it, which at a later stage if I want to, I can sell, or build another property on and rent."

"That's why you have your dad." Dad said. "Because he's a brilliant manager."

I hugged him towards me. "You sure are, Dad." I beamed. "I'm going to go and put an offer in."

Ten minutes later, my offer had been accepted. All my family took it in turns to hug me. I would never be able to do an Ezra and move to another country, away from them. They were too big a part of my life. But thirty minutes away? That suited me just fine.

And the possibility that from time to time I might cross paths with Becca? It never crossed my mind.

I was such a liar.

"Celebration night tonight at bowling." Milo said. "I might even let you use the child ramp or the bumpers, Cal."

"Fuck off."

He chuckled. "What you gonna do about it? You need me more than anyone."

I sighed. "You're going to be a thorn in my side while I get this barn done."

"Hey," he nudged me with his hip. "In all seriousness, I'm looking forward to it. Brother time. Seeing you happier these past days makes me happy. And it takes my mind off the fact that I have to wait to get married. Plus, it gives Vi some time to herself. I know I'm full on."

"Milo Waite is maturing. I'm moving on with my life. What is happening to us both?"

"We're embracing change, bro. Sooner or later it'll happen to the rest of them."

I looked over at the rest of my family and thought about how much I loved them.

"Right, let's get back because I'm ravenous, and we'll be going out again before you know it."

. . .

Back home and in my small bedroom, I considered how much space I would have in the future. It would take months for the barn to be anything approaching liveable and I had to anticipate it could even be a whole year before I got to move in. I could put a caravan on site if I wanted to, but I'd see. Maybe a caravan so I could stay over some nights, like on weekends, and then the rest of the time I'd stay home until I had some rooms that were habitable.

Excitement fizzed in my belly at the thoughts of architect plans, and the idea of a beautiful large home of my own, with enough room in there that should I meet someone, we could have ample space and even have pets. I was still quite focused on the idea of getting a rescue like Vi did, but it wouldn't be fair while I lived alone as I was out at work a lot.

Best to concentrate on the plans I could make come true. My ideal home.

I shrugged on a pair of loose-fitting jeans and a loose t-shirt, so that I had plenty of space to move around. This evening I was determined to come higher up the leaderboard than the bottom two. My male pride was kicking in.

Before long, we were all gathered at the bowling alley, ordering our food and drinks and getting our names up on the scoreboard. It was the usual crew, split across two lanes. All six of us Waites, Violet, Eli and Angela, and Lisa.

Then my mouth dropped when someone I wasn't expecting walked in...

Quinn.

"What the fuck is he doing here?" Jules snapped.

"Good to see you too, Blue."

Blue?

"If I didn't like it so much, I would dye my fucking hair." She said stomping off towards the ladies.

"Quinn, my man. What are you doing here?"

"Thought it was about time I joined the gang. I saw Lisa earlier and she said she'd started coming so I thought I would. I never came before because I thought it was a family thing, but I don't feel so awkward being here if Lisa is too."

Quinn said hello to everyone and then came back to my side.

"I apologise for my sister's behaviour."

"Don't. I enjoy winding her up. It's one of the most exciting parts of my days. Pity this job's just about finished."

"You're a braver man than most, Romeo." I

told him.

"Do not fucking call him that or you can cross my name off your help list." Jules snarled, having just returned from the ladies. Then she looked up. "Anyway, Cal, I think you're going to be otherwise occupied for the rest of the evening."

She nodded towards the end of the lane where Becca had just appeared.

I blinked twice. Was she really here?

"You owe me big time, brother. Big." Jules said, and then she walked towards Becca to hug her.

I just stood there, next to Quinn, frozen in place.

"Oh wow, it's Becca." Quinn said and he too began to walk towards her. Soon everyone was gathered around her, hugging her, and asking her how she was doing. I saw her look my way and she smiled, but I couldn't get near her.

Why was she here?

She said she'd never return to Willowfield in case she encountered any trouble due to Rob's past.

But now she stood right in front of me.

Was she here to make friends with Vi and Jules again?

Jules appeared back at my side. "Before all your usual Cal-crap starts, no she's not here for us. Yes, we're friends again, but she's here because she likes you. You hear me, brother? She. Likes. You. So for God's sake do not mess this up."

"How do you know this?" I asked her.

"I went and plastered her walls. I literally smoothed over the cracks, the surfaces. You and Becca are as bad as each other. She's not interested in anyone else, Cal. Just you. You're on your own now, though. Mess up and you'll have to deal with it. I've enough on avoiding that cretin." She pointed at Quinn.

"He's a nice guy." I told her.

She laughed. "He's okay. But I have as much fun hating him as I do liking him, so I'm going to keep that going a while yet. You give me hope for the future, Cal, but I'm not there yet." She rose onto her tiptoes and kissed my cheek. "Go get her, Cal."

I walked over to Becca and she looked up at me, smiling. "Hey, Cal. You invited me to come, remember? At any time. You said and I quote you'd, 'whoop my arse at bowling'. So it's on." She wiggled her brows.

And just like that, I didn't give two hoots if I lost at bowling, because it looked like I'd just won at life.

CHAPTER TWENTY-FIVE

Becca

I'd never been so nervous in my whole life as I walked into that bowling alley, and I couldn't even say it was because I was scared of being accosted by anyone who remembered I was Rob's widow.

As soon as I'd stepped over to everyone and they'd come and welcomed me with open arms, it was like I'd never been away. But now I had a new challenge and it wasn't to beat Callum at bowling.

It was the fact that we had to stay there, right until the games ended, as most of the people here had no idea that I'd turned up here for Callum.

They thought I'd just come to say hi, after being away for so long.

Or so I'd thought.

But I'd not considered Milo Waite. I listened as Vi updated him about why I was there, and his eyes brightened, and, if I wasn't mistaken, went a bit glassy.

"You like our Cal?" He double-checked.

"I do. And sorry that I made Vi keep that from you, but..."

"Yeah, I'd have told him. She did the right thing on this occasion."

I stared at Vi with wide eyes.

"I know, right. Sometimes now he's not a caveman."

"Huh. I can see my reputation's being threatened." He huffed, and then before I could get an understanding of what was happening, I was upside down.

"What the hell?" I was being lifted by Milo Waite and was currently over his shoulder.

"Welcome to my world." Said Vi.

Then an extremely loud whistle sounded from Milo's mouth. "Callum. Come on, you've got a wench to claim," he shouted at the top of his voice and I could make out the shock on some of the faces present even from my upside-down state.

Cal caught up with us as Milo walked me towards the exit of the bowling alley. Then he put me upright.

"Check your shoes in and then go do whatever you people need to do. I mean sex, in case I'm not clear."

"And your assistance is no longer required, brother." Cal said, looking exasperated.

"Can we fist-bump, bro? This needs a fist-bump. I insist." Milo raised his knuckles.

"I'm not putting out if you don't come sit back down *right now*." Violet shouted at him.

"Jesus, I can never win these days." He sulked, walking off towards her.

I looked at Cal.

He looked at me.

"Shall we get out of here?" He said.

"Want to drive me to mine?" I replied.

On the way back to my house, I told him how I'd come to be there that evening in terms of Juliet's visit and also that I'd paid for a taxi to bring me, even though it had cost a fortune, because it was my intention that Callum Waite would take me home tonight.

And then Callum told me how much he liked me, and how he'd hoped for this night for a long time.

Once we got back to my house there was no room for talking anymore. Unless it was for expressions like, 'oh God'.

As Callum carried me upstairs, my insides were bursting with butterflies. It had been a long, long time, and for years there had just been Rob.

Cal placed me gently down on my bed and then pulling me onto my side next to him, his lips met mine and It. Was. Everything.

Fireworks. Mini explosions. Jolts of electricity.

All whirled within me as I took in the new sensations that Cal created within me.

He kissed me for the longest time. We'd taken so long to get here, years if you thought about our first meeting where fate had diverted our paths, and now we were in no rush.

Our hands ran all over the other's body, learning each part of our new lover, and then Callum began to move and took his time kissing my skin. Down my neck, across my collarbone and on.

Now was a new beginning, and I saw it as Callum wiping away every trace of my past as he kissed a new place.

And then he moved my thighs apart and kissed my pussy.

"Ohhh." I raised my thighs to meet his moves.

I didn't feel in any way awkward being so intimate with Callum after all this time of knowing him as a friend. It just felt so right. As if finally fate had altered the jigsaw of my life and put the right pieces in it to fix together. To complete me.

Soon Callum came back up the bed and no more words were said between us as his cock nudged at my heat. We were both clean and I knew there was no risk of pregnancy. His mouth fixed on mine as he slipped inside me and then he moved slowly back and forth while we got used to each other.

We were lost in sensations until Cal deepened his thrusts and I met them seeking completion. When it came it was heaven. I trembled around him as I felt his own release.

"Fuck, that was everything." He whispered in my ear, before biting on my lobe.

We spent the rest of the night and the early hours of the morning acquainting ourselves with each other's bodies and when I woke up the next morning tangled around Cal, I just knew that we would be okay. That the path ahead might pose challenges, but there was nothing Cal and I couldn't face... together.

CHAPTER TWENTY-SIX

Callum

The night (and some of the morning) had been amazing. Once we'd showered together and had breakfast, I drove Becca to see my new place, although we could only look from outside without the estate agent.

"It's incredible." She said, her arm linked through mine. "So you reckon it could be a year though until it's done?"

"Yeah, but I'm going to put a caravan on site while I renovate. Spend some time staying over and some time at home. Hopefully having an amazing team behind me can get it done quicker and I'll employ other tradesmen. It's too much for just my family to do. The more people I have here, the quicker it's done; and I'll be honest, I can't wait to move in."

"The garden is going to be huge." She paused. "Laurel would go wild here. Our garden is small as you know. Is it available for rent by the hour?" She laughed.

"Becca." I sat on a wall at the edge of the property. "I know it's extremely early days, but I just want you to know. I'm serious about you..."

She took a deep inhale. "I feel the same way, Cal. It's mad, isn't it?"

I shrugged. "I don't care, it's amazing. And you and Laurel can come here any time you like as long as it's safe to do so."

"Thank you."

I took a deep breath. " I know you've done all this marriage stuff before and it must be difficult to imagine trusting someone again, especially with Laurel, and that's fine with me. But if we're still together the day this house is fully ready, I will ask you to move in."

Becca smiled.

"And either you do, or we stay living between two properties. Either works for me. I'm not my brother; I don't need everything right now. I can wait, until you're ready."

She stood between my knees and looked down at me. "When this house is fully ready, I will seriously consider *whatever* questions you ask me."

I understood the hidden meaning to her words and my heart thudded in my chest. "That makes me a very happy man."

"And I'm a very happy woman. You just need to make sure I stay that way." She quipped. I pulled her down so that her lips met mine. "That's a good start." She whispered against my mouth.

I groaned, resting my forehead against hers. I wanted her again, but that wasn't an option right now.

"Shall we go and pick Laurel up and take her to the park? Tell her you're Mummy's new boyfriend?" Becca asked.

"I'd like that." I began to stand, rubbing at my butt that had been resting on the cold bricks of the wall.

"And you can meet my parents and face my father's questions and my mother's nosiness."

"I'm okay with that too." I gave her a cheesy grin.

"You do know Laurel will ask if you're going to be her daddy, right? Might be today, might be tomorrow, but at some point she'll ask." Becca said hesitantly.

"And how does Laurel's mummy suggest I answer that question?" I prompted.

She grabbed hold of my hand. "How about you say that right now you're still Cal, but maybe one day you might be?"

I smiled so hard it almost broke my face.

"I think that answer would be perfect."

CHAPTER TWENTY-SEVEN

Callum

I'd survived meeting Becca's parents. They were as lovely as Becca and I could see how close she was to them. We'd reassured them by saying we were taking things slow. Laurel was excited that she'd be seeing more of me, but as a three-year-old it mainly centred around what toys she wanted to show me and what we could play.

Although I wanted nothing more than to spend every minute of my spare time with Becca, it wasn't fair on Laurel and so we'd agreed that we'd see each other twice in the week and then on a week-end. All except the approaching weekend when I'd be in London at the premiere of Ezra's new film. Soon I'd be busy renovating my new home anyway, so all in all it would work well.

Ezra was due to arrive at any moment after saying he wanted to spend a couple of days here before heading off to the capital. As Ezra texted that he was turning the corner of the street, Eli made me go outside the front of the house with him to greet him.

"Oh my god, Eli. Alright then." I looked skyward and then back at my dad and Angela, who both laughed.

As I stood outside, I realised it was a lot cooler than I thought.

"Won't be a sec, Eli. Just going to grab my jumper from the kitchen." I'd left it on the back of the chair at lunch as the kitchen had got warm.

"Oh, fuck, sorry." I spluttered as I pushed open the kitchen door to find my dad and Angela in a passionate embrace.

"Shit." My dad said, exchanging a glance with Angela. "Cal—"

"It's fine with me, but we don't have time for this now. Ezra's taxi is just pulling up." I went back outside. "It might be nice if you come greet him too, Dad, though."

"Yes, yes, of course." Dad and Angela began to follow me, no doubt red-faced.

I made my way outside, watching as my brother emerged from the taxi. I could just make out, due to the winter sunshine, that there was someone else in the back of the car with him.

As he walked over towards us, his face didn't show the expression I expected. The one of happiness at greeting us all.

"I'm sorry, Dad." He said, turning to face him. "I didn't have any choice. She came with me or said she'd turn up on her own. I figured it was better this way."

And then the other passenger of the car exited and walked towards us. A bob-haired, bottle blonde with an aged complexion, but a Hollywood smile.

She walked right up to Ezra's side.

"Hello, Josh." She said to my dad. "Surprise."

"Hello, Alice." He replied tersely and I heard Angela gasp.

Me? I was still trying to get my head around the fact that my long-lost mother was standing on the doorstep.

THE END

The secrets of Ezra's past will be revealed in Acting on Love

ABOUT ANGEL

Angel Devlin is the contemporary romance penname of paranormal/suspense writer, Andie M. Long. Check out Angel for stories as hot as her coffee.

She lives in Sheffield with her partner, son, and a gorgeous whippet called Bella.

Newsletter:

Sign up to Angel/Andie's newsletter here for exclusive content.

www.subscribepage.com/f8v2u5

THE WAITE BROTHERS SERIES

Fix my Heart

A Second Spark

Acting on Love

Printed in Great Britain
by Amazon

11731561R00164